The Secret Life Of Amy Bensen

Book 1: Escaping Reality
By Lisa Renee Jones
Copyright 2013

Infinite possibilities...
Infinite passion...
Infinite danger...

His touch spirals through me, warm and sweet, wicked and hot. I shouldn't trust him. I shouldn't tell him my secrets. But how do I not when is the reason I breathe. He is what I need.

Chapter One

$$\pi$$

A my...
My name is all that is written on the plain white envelope taped to the mirror.

I step out of the stall inside the bathroom of Manhattan's Metropolitan Museum, and the laughter and joy of the evening's charity event I've been enjoying fades away. Fear and dread slam into me, shooting adrenaline through my body. No. No. No. This cannot be happening and yet it is. It is, and I know what it means. Suddenly, the room begins to shift and everything goes gray. I fight the flashback I haven't had in years, but I am already right there in it, in the middle of a nightmare. The scent of smoke burns my nose. The sound of blistering screams shreds my nerves. There is pain and heartache, and the loss of all I once had and will never know again. Fighting a certain meltdown, I swallow hard and shove away the gut-wrenching memories. I can't let this happen. Not here, not in a public place. Not when I'm quite certain danger is knocking on my door.

On wobbly knees and four-inch, black strappy heels that had made me feel sexy only minutes before and clumsy now, I step forward and press my palms to the counter. I can't seem to make myself reach for the envelope and my gaze goes to my image in the mirror, to my long white-blond hair I've worn draped around my shoulders tonight rather than tied at my nape, and done so as a proud reflection of the heritage of my Swedish mother I'm tired of denying. Gone too are the dark-rimmed glasses I've often used to hide the pale blue eyes both of my parents had shared, making it too easy for me to see the empty shell of a person I've become. If this is what I am at twenty-four years old, what I will be like at thirty-four?

Voices sound outside the doorway and I yank the envelope from the mirror and rush into the stall, sealing myself inside. Still chatting, two females enter the bathroom, and I tune out their gossip about some man they'd admired at the party. I suddenly need to confirm my fate. Leaning against the wall, I open the sealed envelope to remove a plain white note card and a key drops to the floor that looks like it goes to a locker. Cursing my shaking hand, I bend down and scoop it up. For a moment, I can't seem to stand up. I want to be strong. I shove to my feet and blink away the burning sensation in my eyes to read the few short sentences typed on the card.

I've found you and so can they. Go to JFK Airport directly. Do not go home. Do not linger. Locker 111 will have everything you need.

My heart thunders in my chest as I take in the signature that is nothing more than a triangle with some writing inside of it. It's the tattoo that had been worn on the arm of the stranger who I'd met only once before. He'd saved my life and helped me restart a new one, and he'd made sure I knew that symbol meant that I am in danger and I have to run.

I squeeze my eyes shut, fighting a wave of emotions. Once again, my life is about to be turned upside down. Once again, I will lose everything, and while everything is so much less than before, it's all I have. I crumble the note in my hand, desperate to make it, and this hell that is my reality, go away. After six years of hiding, I'd dared to believe I could find "normal", but that was a mistake. Deep down, I've known that since two months ago when I'd left my job at the central library as a research assistant, to work at the museum. Being here is treading water too close to the bridge.

Straightening, I listen as the women's voices fade before the room goes silent. Anger erupts inside me at the idea that my life is about to be stolen from me again and I tear the note in tiny pieces, flush them down the toilet and shove the envelope into the trash. I want to throw away the key too, but some part of me won't let that happen. Probably the smart, unemotional part of me that I hate right now.

Unzipping the small black purse I have strapped across my chest and over my pale blue blazer, that despite my tight budget, I'd splurged on for this new job; I drop the key inside, sealing it away. I'm going to finish my party. Maybe I'm going to finish my life right here in New York City. The note didn't say I'd been found. It only warned me that I could be found. I don't want to run again. I don't. I need time to think, to process, and that is going to have to wait until after the party.

Decision made, I exit the stall, cutting my eyes away from the mirror and heading for the door. I do not want anyone to see me right now when I have no idea who "me" is or will be tomorrow. In a zone, that numb place I've used as a survival tool almost as many times as I've tried to find the meaning of that symbol on the note, I follow the soft hum of orchestra music from well-placed speakers, entering a room with a high oval ceiling decorated with magnificent artwork. I tell myself to get lost in the crush of patrons in business attire, while waiters toting trays offer champagne and finger foods, but I don't. I simply stand there, mourning the new life I've just begun, and I know is now gone. My "zone" has failed me.

"Where have you been?"

The question comes as Chloe Monroe, the only person I've let myself consider a friend in years, steps in front of me, a frown on her heart-shaped face. From her dark brown curls bouncing around her shoulders to her outgoing personality and fun, flirty attitude, she is my polar opposite and I love that about her. She is everything I am not but hoped I would become. Now I will lose her. Now I will lose me again.

"Well," she prods when I don't reply quickly enough, shoving her hands onto her hips, "Where have you been?"

LISA RENEE JONES

"Bathroom," I say. "There was a line." I sound awkward. I feel awkward. I hate how easily the lie comes to me, how it defines me. A lie is all that I am.

Chloe's brow puckers. "Hmmm. There wasn't one when I was there. I guess I got lucky." She waves off the thought. "Sabrina is freaking out over some donation paperwork she can't find and says she needs you." Her brow furrows. "I thought you were doing research? When did you start handling donor paperwork?"

"Last week, when she got overwhelmed," I say, and perk up at the idea that my new boss needs me. I don't need to leave. I need to be needed even if it's just for tonight. "Where is she?"

"By the front desk." She laces her arm through mine. "And I'm tagging along with you. I have a sixty-year-old admirer who's bordering on stalker. I need to hide before he hunts me down."

She tugs me forward, and I let her, too distracted by her words to stop her. She's worried about being hunted but I am the one being hunted. I thought I wasn't anymore. I thought I was safe, but I am never safe, and neither is anyone around me. I've lived that first-hand. I felt that heartache of loss, and while being alone sucks, losing someone you care about is far worse.

My selfishness overwhelms me and I stop dead in my tracks to pull Chloe around to face me. "Tell Sabrina I'm grabbing the forms and will be right there."

"Oh. Yes. Okay." Chloe lets go of my arm, and for a moment I fight the urge to hug her, but that would make her seem important to me, and someone could be watching. I turn away from her and rush for a door, and I feel sick to my stomach knowing that I will never see her again.

I finally exit the side of the building into the muggy August evening, and head for a line of cabs, but I do not rush or look around me. I've learned ways to avoid attention, and going to work for a place that has a direct link to the world I'd left behind hadn't been one of them. It had simply been a luxury I'm now paying for.

6

"JFK Airport," I pant as I slide into the back of a cab, and rub the back of my neck at a familiar prickling sensation. A feeling I'd had often my first year on my own, when I'd been certain danger waited for me around every corner. Hunted. I'm being hunted. All the denial I own won't change my reality.

**

The ride to the airport is thirty minutes and it takes me another fifteen to figure out what terminal locker 111 is in once I'm inside the building. I pull it open and there is a carry-on-sized roller suitcase and a smaller brown leather shoulder bag with a large yellow envelope sticking up from inside the open zipper. I have no desire to be watched while I explore what's been left for me. I remove the locker's contents, and follow a sign that indicates a bathroom.

Once again in a stall, I pull down the baby changer and check the contents of the envelope on top. There is a file folder, a bankcard, a cell phone, a passport, a note card, and another small sealed envelope. I reach for the note first.

There is cash in the bank account and the code is 1850. I'll add more as you need it until you get fully settled. You'll find a new social security card, driver's license, and passport as well. You have a complete history to memorize and a résumé and job history that will check out if looked into. Throw out your cell phone. The new one is registered under your new name and address. There's a plane ticket and the keys to an apartment along with a location. Toss all identification and don't use your bank account or credit cards. Be smart. Don't link yourself to your past. Stay away from museums this time.

A new name. That's what stands out to me. I'm getting another new name. No. No. No. My heart races at the idea. I don't want another new name. Even more than I don't want to be back on the run, I don't want another new name. I feel like a girl having her hair chopped off. I'm losing part of myself. After living a lie for years, I'm losing the only part of my fake identity I'd ever really accepted as me.

LISA RENEE JONES

I grab the passport and flip it open and my hand trembles at the sight of a photo that is a present-day me. How did this stranger I met only one time in my life get a picture of me this recent? It doesn't matter that I'd once considered him my guardian angel. I'm freaked out by this. Has he been watching me all this time? I shiver at the idea, and my only comfort is my new name. I'm now Amy Bensen rather than Amy Reynolds. I'm still Amy. It is the one piece of good news in all of this and I cling to it, using it to stave off the meltdown I feel coming. I just have to hold it together until I get on the plane. Then I can sink into my seat and think myself into my "zone" that I can't seem to fully find.

Flipping open the folder, I find an airline ticket. I'm going to Denver and I leave in an hour. I've never been anywhere but Texas and New York. All I know about Denver is it's big, cold, and the next place I will pretend is home when I have no home. The thought makes my chest pinch, but fear of what might await me if I don't run pushes me past it.

I turn off my cell phone so it won't ping and stuff it, with everything but my new ID and plane ticket, back into the envelope. I have my own money in the bank and I'm not about to get rid of my identification and access to that resource. Besides, the idea of using a bankcard that allows me to be tracked bothers me. I'll be visiting the bank tomorrow and removing any cash I can get my hands on. When I'd been eighteen, naive and alone, I'd blindly trusted a stranger I'd called my guardian angel. I might have to trust him now too, but it won't be blindly.

Making my way to check in, I fumble through using the ticket machine and my new identification and then track a path to security. A few minutes later, I'm on the other side of the metal detectors and I stop at a store to buy random things I might need. All is going well until I arrive at the ticket counter.

"I'm so sorry, Ms. Bensen," the forty-something woman begins. "We had an administrative error and seats were double-booked. We—"

8

"I have to be on this flight," I say in a hissed whisper with my heart in my throat. "I have to be on this flight."

"I can get you a voucher and the first flight tomorrow."

"No. No. Tonight. Give someone a bigger voucher to get me a seat."

"I—"

"Talk to a supervisor," I insist, because while avoiding attention means I am not a pushy person, and despite my initial denial of my circumstances that might suggest otherwise, I have no death wish. I am alive and plan to stay that way.

She purses her lips and looks like she might argue, but finally she turns away and makes a path toward a man in uniform. Their heads dip low and he glances at me before the woman returns. "We have you on standby and we'll try to get you on."

"How likely is it you'll get me on?"

"We're going to try."

"Try how hard?"

Her lips purse again. "Very."

I let out a sigh of relief. "Thank you. And I'm sorry. I have a…crisis of sorts. I really have to get to my destination." There is a thread of desperation to my voice I do not contain well.

Her expression softens and I know she heard it. "I understand and I am sorry this happened," she assures me. "We are trying to make this right and so you don't panic please know that we have to get everyone boarded before we make any passenger changes. You'll likely be the last on the plane."

"Thanks," I say, feeling awkward. "I'll just go sit." Definitely flustered, I turn away from the counter. Ignoring the few vacant seats, I head to the window and settle my bags on the floor beside me. Leaning against the steel handrail on the glass, I position myself to see everyone around me to be sure I'm prepared for any problem before it's on me. And that's when the room falls away, when my gaze collides with his.

He is sitting in a seat that faces me, one row between us, his features handsomely carved, his dark hair a thick, rumpled finger temptation. He's dressed in faded jeans and a dark blue t-shirt,

LISA RENEE JONES

but he could just as easily be wearing a finely fitted suit and tie. He is older than me, maybe thirty, but there is a worldliness, a sense of control and confidence, about him that reaches beyond years. He is money, power, and sex, and while I cannot make out the color of his eyes, I don't need to. All that matters is that he is one hundred percent focused on me, and me on him. A moment ago, I was alone in a crowd and suddenly, I'm with him. As if the space between us is nothing. I tell myself to look away, that everyone is a potential threat, but I just...can't.

His eyes narrow the tiniest bit, and then his lips curve ever so slightly and I am certain I see satisfaction slide over his face. He knows I cannot look away. I've become his newest conquest, of which I am certain he has many, and I've embarrassingly done so without one single moan of pleasure in the process.

"Inviting our first-class guests to board now," a female voice says over the intercom.

I blink and my new, hmmm, whatever he is, pushes to his feet and slides a duffle onto his shoulder. His eyes hold mine, a hint of something in them I can't quite make out. Challenge, I think. Challenge? What kind of challenge? I don't have time to figure it out. He turns away, and just like that, I'm alone again.

Chapter Two

Everyone has boarded the plane but me. I am alone in the gate area aside from a few airline personnel, and I feel vulnerable and exposed with no crowd to hide me. I'm already thinking through my options for the evening if I don't make this flight, when my new name is called. "Your lucky day, Ms. Bensen," the attendant says as I approach the counter. "You've been bumped to first class."

I blink in surprise, and not just at the oddity of being called Ms. Bensen. "Are you sure? First class?"

"That's right."

"How much extra?" I ask, unsure of how much money I have on the card I've been given, unable to use my personal savings for fear of being tracked. I'm not even sure the little bit my extra holiday jobs allowed me would cover it.

"No cost to you," she assures me, smiling and motioning to my ticket. "Let me fix your paperwork so you can hurry along before they seal the doors and you still miss your flight."

"Yes," I say quickly. "Thank you."

I rush down the walkway to my flight, and despite my relief at scoring a seat, the realness of leaving New York punches me in the gut. Everything I've come to know as my world is here and I haven't felt this helpless since…a long time ago. I can't think about what happened. I don't think about it. That's when the nightmares start, and so does the fear. This isn't the time to let the terror control me. I have no idea what I will face in the next few hours and days.

"Welcome aboard," a flight attendant says cheerfully as I reach the plane, and somehow I muster a half-smile before making my way to row seven, where there are only two seats. My aisle assignment is empty as expected, and—impossibly, after they've told me the airline was overbooked—the one by the window also appears empty. Hope that I might be alone is dashed when I note the bag stored beneath the seat, which tells me my companion is nearby. I sigh. It would suit me just fine to slip into my leather seat and shut my eyes before whomever it is returns, but alas, that's simply not an option. I have luggage to store and a file to study.

With a shrug, I let the oversized bag hanging from my shoulder fall into my intended seat, then push the handle down on my new roller suitcase. Grimacing, I discover the bin above me is full. Apparently, nothing is going to be easy tonight. Pushing to my toes, I try to adjust some bags to make room for mine, and it's as much a struggle as breathing is right now.

"Let me help you."

The deep, slightly husky male voice has me turning to my left to find myself captured in a familiar stare. My heart sputters. It can't be. But it is. I've made a fool of myself by gaping at a gorgeous man and he's here to make me pay in buckets of embarrassment. The man from the terminal is standing beside me, towering over my five feet three inches by close to a foot, and standing so close that I no longer have to guess the color of his eyes. They are blue, a piercing aqua blue that is almost green, and they are once again focused one hundred percent on me.

"I…ah…thank you."

"My pleasure," he says, a quirk to his mouth that I am once again looking at, along with the dark stubble shadowing his strong jaw along with his barely there goatee, which makes me think pirate. The kind that steals a girl's senses and ravishes her body, leaving her incapable of anything but a whimper as she watches him walk out the door. Mr. Tall, Dark and Potentially Dangerous reaches over me to adjust the compartment, his t-shirt stretching over a perfectly sculpted broad chest. I don't move—me, a person who believes wholeheartedly in personal space. I know I should and I mean to, but I don't seem to have control over my legs, let alone anything else tonight.

He glances down at me, still shifting my luggage. "Just this bag?" he asks, and there is heat in his eyes. Or maybe amusement. And conquest, definitely conquest, which must get old for a man like him.

The thought is enough to make me step back, probably a bit too obviously. "Yes. Thank you." Arms still stretched over his head, he adjusts my bag, muscles flexing, long torso stretching deliciously, and I don't try to look away. Admiring this man keeps me from thinking about the hundreds of other people on this flight that could be trouble.

"We're all set," he says, motioning to the seat. "You want the window?"

"Window?" My belly tightens and I feel breathless. "We're seated together?"

"Appears that way." Humor lights his eyes, and his mouth that I am somehow looking at, quirks as he adds, "Small world."

My cheeks heat at the reference to our little encounter in the terminal. "Too small," I say, and an announcement over the intercom urges us to sit, saving me from some witty comment I don't have.

"Last chance," he says. "Window?"

I open myself to decline and snap my mouth shut. An aisle seat exposes me to the other passengers, many at my back. The only person who will ravish me while I'm trapped between this man and the wall is this man. "Do you mind?"

"Not at all."

"Thank you," I say, before I grab my bag and move to the seat he's just given up, only to remember that he'd been settled here before I arrived. "Do you want your things from under the seat?"

13

He slides in beside me and he is big, and broad and too good-looking for the safety of womankind. "Why don't I just put yours under my seat?" he suggests.

He smells spicy and masculine, and the scent stirs a distant memory in the back of my mind. I shove it away, frustrated that I'm back to every little thing triggering flashbacks. Today has undone the strength I'd spent years creating in myself, made me weak as I once was. "Yes," I agree. "Just let me grab a few things for the flight." I quickly remove my file and my purse and hand over my carry-on, and in the process, my hand brushes his. A jolt of electricity darts up my arm and I quickly turn away, buckling myself in. Maybe being locked in a corner with a man I am powerless to control my reactions to isn't so smart.

"Champagne?"

I glance up to find a pretty twenty-something flight attendant holding a tray and gobbling up my seating partner with unabashed approval that makes me think of the bold way Chloe lives her life, and suddenly it's hard to breathe. I will never see Chloe again.

"Why yes, we will," my travel partner says, accepting two glasses, and turning to me, successfully dismissing the flight attendant.

I hold up a hand. "No. Thank you."

"We have a designated driver."

"I'm afraid it will make me sleepy," I object, though I am certain the visit from my guardian angel, or handler, has ensured I won't rest well again for a very long time.

"It's a four-hour flight," he points out. "Sleepy isn't a bad thing."

Sleepy. This gorgeous, incredibly masculine man has just said "sleepy" and it seems so out of the realm of what I expect from him, that he has managed the impossible considering my life right now. I smile an honest smile and accept the glass. "I suppose it's not." I sip the sweet, bubbly beverage.

A glint of satisfaction flickers in his eyes, as if he's pleased I've done as he wishes, before he takes my glass from me and sets both our drinks in the cup holders between us. The easy way he assumes control of my tiniest actions, and seems to enjoy doing so, should bother me. For reasons I don't have time to analyze, it only makes him more tantalizingly male.

He extends his hand. "Liam Stone."

My pulse jumps at both his ridiculously alluring name and the idea of touching him. I start to lift my hand and hesitate with the oddest sense of this moment changing my life in some way. Pushing past the crazy thought, I press my palm to his. "Nice to meet you, Liam. I'm Amy."

His fingers close around mine and a slow, warm, tingling sensation slides up my arm. "Tell me what I did to make you smile so I can do it again." His voice is low, gravelly. As sexy as the man who owns it. I expect him to let go of me, but his fingers seem to flex around my hand, tightening as if he doesn't want to let go. I am shocked at how much I, someone who avoids people I do not know well, do not want him to.

"Sleepy," I manage, and my voice sounds as affected as I suddenly, or maybe not so suddenly, feel.

His brows furrow. "Sleepy?"

"That's what you said that made me smile. You don't seem like a man who'd say 'sleepy'."

He arches a brow and he's still holding my hand. I should object. I should pull away. Because he has the experience and depth, I've long avoided and craved in a man. All I succeed in doing is melting into my chair, like I know I could easily melt for him. "Is that so?" he challenges.

"Yes. That's so."

He looks amused, and—reluctantly, it seems—he releases my hand. Or maybe not reluctantly. Maybe he wasn't holding it as long as it felt like he was holding it. I fear I have no concept of what is real anymore.

Liam leans closer, so close it's like he plans to share a secret, and still I want him closer. "Just what kind of man do you think I am, Amy?"

The kind that flirts with lost little girls who don't even know their own names and then darts off to see the world with a supermodel, I think, but I say, "Not the kind who says 'sleepy'."

Laughter rumbles from his chest, a deep, masculine sound that spreads warmth through my body. Impossibly, it is both fire in my veins and balm for my nerves, calming me in an unexplainable way, when I know he is too good looking, too inquisitive, and absolutely too controlling to play with. Not that I would even know how to play with a man like this, or really, any man for that matter. Men, like friends, have been risky propositions.

"Why are you headed to Denver, Amy?" he asks, and the soothing balm becomes shards of glass splintering through me.

"Excuse me," the flight attendant thankfully interrupts, saving me an answer that is still in a file I haven't read. "Can I take your dinner orders?"

"Chicken," I say.

Liam glances at me. "How do you know they have chicken?"

"It's the go-to food for hotels, parties, and airlines." And there was a time in my youth when all those things had been in my life. I glance at the flight attendant for confirmation, and she nods. "Chicken it is."

"Make that two orders of chicken," Liam says with another rumbling of that deeply addictive laughter of his, and while I like his easygoing nature, I can almost feel the band of control he pulls around him. A muffled ringing sound fills the air.

"Whoever is ringing," the flight attendant warns, "you have about one minute until electronic devices are off."

She rushes away, and since the sound is obviously coming from Liam's bag, I cautiously adjust my skirt and bend over to grab it, dislodging my folder in the process. My heart lurches as it tumbles to the ground and spills open, the contents flying everywhere. I grab for the contents, shoving papers inside the folder again as quickly as I can.

"Your résumé, I believe," Liam says, and I freeze at his obvious nosy inspection of the document I have yet to read. The idea that he knows more about me than me is unnerving. Slowly, I lift my gaze to find only a few inches separating us, and his eyes, those piercing blue eyes, see too much. He makes me feel too much. I don't know him. I can't trust him. Is there anyone I can really trust left in this world?

"Thanks," I say, taking the resume from him with more obvious snap than I intend. I tug his bag out from underneath my seat. He unzips the side pocket to remove his phone, and I am self-conscious of how high my skirt rides up my thigh as he helps me shove the bag back where it had been. But he isn't looking at my legs. I can feel the burn of him watching me in my cheeks. I know he knows how uncomfortable I am. I know he knows I'm not okay right now. I feel trapped. Trapped with this man, and I am trapped in a life that isn't mine.

Tugging at my skirt, I sit up and he does the same, shifting his attention to his phone as he does. Taking advantage of his distraction, I twist toward the window, offering him my back. Maybe he will think I'm allowing him privacy for his call. Maybe he will think I'm rude. I don't care. I open the folder and quickly find the résumé he's already seen and start reading. Amy Bensen is, or was, a private secretary to some executive, whose name I quickly press to memory. She's had that job since graduating college three years before, but he's retired and she's been laid off.

I flip to a summary page behind the résumé that tells me my back-story, and read on, hearing Liam talking on his phone about some meeting. An announcement is made about electronic items and I read faster. Amy Bensen has scored a three-month position handling the personal affairs of a private businessman who is both a friend of her ex-boss and overseas for that time period. Her new boss will be providing an apartment near his personal home that is empty and will need to be monitored. There is a comment typed in bold and underlined. You are not to apply for work until I contact you and tell you that it's safe. Do nothing to bring attention to yourself. I inhale a slow, heavy breath and can't seem to let it out. Until I tell you it's safe? What does that even mean? Who is after me? Do they, or he or she, or whoever, know I was

17

in New York? Can they figure out where I went? And why, why, why have I let myself pretend this threat doesn't exist until I'm forced into hiding again?

The plane roars to life and I nearly jump out of my skin. Casting a glance over my shoulder, I confirm that Liam didn't notice, and is concentrating on punching something into his phone. He might not be attentive to me right now but he already started asking me questions. He'll ask more and I have to be ready. Thumbing through the file, I find a page with my new family history. My mother died in a car accident four years ago and my father was a drunk who left us when I was a kid. I have no siblings. A wave of nausea overcomes me and I shut the file, and still facing the window, I lie back against the seat, squeezing my eyes shut. I'd adored my mother. I'd worshiped my older brother. And my father would never have left me by choice. I had a family that was more than a typed piece of paper in a file. Now I have nothing but a fake name and a fake life.

Chapter Three

We level off at cruising altitude, the soft hum of the engines lulling me into deep thought, and I can feel my mind trying to go places I don't want to go. Flashes of the tattoo on my handler's wrist keep interrupting my plans to keep Liam's questions at bay the rest of the flight. The tattoo shifts to flames and I am suddenly floating in a cloud of thick smoke, trying to escape, but I can't see to get out of it. I can't scream. I try to scream. They are screaming. Oh God. Oh God. I have to get to them. A sudden bright light pierces the fog and I jerk to a sitting position and grab my throat, gasping for air, feeling the rasp of smoke burn through my lungs.

"Easy, sweetheart. You're okay."

I barely register the voice. I can't focus. My hands go to my face. "Where am I?"

"Amy."

Strong hands touch me, turn me, and I blink a pair of piercing blue eyes into focus. Memories rush over me. "Liam?"

"Yes. Liam. That must have been one hell of a nightmare."

Nightmare? I fell asleep? "No, I…" Images flash in my mind, and I squeeze my eyes shut, trying to block out my fear, the smoke, and gut wrenching screams. My fingers curl around what I realize is Liam's shirt, and on some level I know that I'm clinging to a man I barely know, but he is all I have. Somehow, he is all that is keeping me from melting down.

"Amy," Liam whispers, stroking a hand down my hair. I tell myself it's inappropriate for him to touch me like this. It's also exactly what I need, and somehow so is he. I tell myself it's simply that he's at the right place at this very wrong time in my life, but it does nothing to discourage my reaction to his touch, to the warmth radiating from where my palms rest on his chest and up my arms. Without a conscious decision, I lean closer to him and my lashes lift, my eyes meeting his, and the connection shoots adrenaline through me. I am no longer in the hell of my head. I am right here with this man and he leaves no room for anything else.

"Is she okay?"

I jerk back at the sound of the flight attendant's voice and Liam's hands fall away from me, leaving me oddly cold. "Excuse me? Am I okay?" I ask, wondering what the heck I did that would merit that question.

"She doesn't like it when I talk sports," Liam jokes, obviously trying to spare me a more personal explanation of…what? What the heck did I do?

"Too much basketball makes me crazy," I add, trying to snatch up the breadcrumbs Liam has tossed my way, but I fear I sound too strained to sound more than baffled.

"It's not basketball season," she points out, looking less than pleased.

"Since when does that stop a basketball fan from killing us with basketball talk?" I ask, and that earns me a deadpan look, which has me quickly shifting gears, trying to make blind amends. "I'm fine. Sorry if I caused some kind of trouble."

She frowns and glowers accusingly at Liam, and all signs of her admiration of his overwhelmingly hotness from earlier are gone. "She doesn't seem fine." Her gaze shifts to me. "You shouted. It scared the heck out of us."

Shouted? Oh, good grief. Way to not bring attention to yourself, Amy. "I took a decongestant," I say, trying to be truly convincing this time. "They make me sleepy and give me nightmares."

Her lips purse, but her expression quickly softens. "Well, that makes sense. Yes. I can see how that might happen to someone sensitive to medications, but boy oh boy they must have worked you over. We've only been in the air fifteen minutes and you were awake when we took off. You were knocked out hard and fast."

Which isn't like me. Not on a normal day. Certainly not on a day I feel threatened. "I'm really sorry I scared you," I offer, attempting a smile that I'm pretty sure never makes it to my lips. "I promise to stay awake the rest of the flight."

"You don't have to promise that," she says, and grins. "But maybe warn us before you go to sleep. We'll have dinner served in five minutes." She rushes away and Liam doesn't give me time to savor her departure.

"Decongestants?" Liam asks softly, drawing my gaze back to his.

"My ears pop when I fly." The lie comes easily. I'm back to the me I hate. "And unless you want to confess to drugging me, that's my story and I'm sticking with it."

He studies me a bit too carefully for my own good, and something in his eyes has me warm all over and wishing he'd touch me again. "What are you afraid of, Amy?"

You, I want to say. You scare me because you make me want to trust you. I laugh, and it sounds strained even to my own ears. "Godzilla," I say, confessing the fictional monster I'd feared in childhood, until life had shown me real monsters existed.

If I'd expected his laughter, he doesn't give it to me. "Godzilla?" he prods, angling his body to block out anyone passing by us, his back to them, his body almost caging mine. The impact of this man's full attention is overwhelming. My breath turns shallow, and to my utter disbelief, my nipples are tight and achy. I do not respond to men like this. I just...don't.

"Everyone has a proverbial monster under the bed," I manage, and thankfully, my voice sounds far more steady than I feel. "Godzilla is mine," I continue. "And hey—at least there weren't any hippos crossing the road in this nightmare. I've had that one a time or two, as well. Actually, I don't think the hippos felt like nightmares. Just strange dreams." Shut up, Amy. Shut up. Why are you telling him anything more than you have to? You never, ever tell more than you have to.

"I won't try to analyze what the hippos mean," he comments, and the slight curve to his lips on the words fades away as he adds, "but your monster under the bed sounds more like a skeleton in the closet to me."

"Fear and a secret are two different things," I remind him, pointing out the difference in the two phrases.

"Often they come together. A secret that leads to fear in one way, shape, or form."

Suddenly, my joke feels like an open window to my soul that I desperately want to slam shut. Tension coils in my muscles and I quickly pull my guard into place, turning the tables. "Sounds like a man who speaks from experience."

"Yes, well," he says, a cynical tinge to his voice, "experience isn't all it's cracked up to be, now is it?"

I search his eyes and look for the meaning behind his words, but I find nothing. He is unreadable, as guarded as I am on my best day, and I sense that I've now glimpsed a little piece of his soul. "What makes you have nightmares, Liam?"

"Nothing." His answer is short and fast, his tone as unreadable as his face remains.

"Everyone has something that scares them."

"I own my fear. It doesn't own me."

A sound of disbelief slips from my throat. "You make it sound so easy to control fear." I regret the words that admit my fear the instant I speak them. It's a mistake I never make, but I've made it with him. Liam truly is dangerous.

His gaze lowers to my mouth, lingering there and sending a tingling sensation down my neck and over my breasts, before slowly lifting. "Maybe you haven't had the right teacher, Amy."

What did that even mean, and why did it create an acute throb between my legs? I'm spiraling out of control and my defenses bristle. "I didn't say I needed a teacher."

"You didn't say you didn't, either."

"Dinner is served," the flight attendant announces, and neither of us looks at her.

"I don't," I say, and now I'm the one who isn't sure if I'm trying to convince him or me. My heart is racing. Why is my heart racing?

His lips quirk. "If you say so."

"Dinner is served," the flight attendant repeats, sounding a little anxious.

"I do say so," I assure him, cutting my gaze and lowering my tray to have my chicken dinner immediately placed on top of it.

The flight attendant leaves us alone and I don't look at Liam. I have this sense that if I do, he'll see more of me than I see myself. As it is, I'm letting him see things I shouldn't have. This banter between us has to stop. It will stop. No more. I'm done playing friendly seatmate. There is a reason I stay away from men like Liam, men with experience and confidence. Men who make a girl who already can't remember her name forget her name. They do see too much. And they make everyone else see too little.

I snatch a roll from my plate that I don't want and tear it apart, then set it back down. Teacher. What does that even mean? And why am I making myself crazy wondering, anyway? It doesn't matter. He'll be out of my life in a few short, or not so short, hours. And true to that assessment, the next few minutes feel like an eternity. I tell myself the silence is good. We are slipping into a typical passenger-to-passenger travel arrangement. We don't have to talk. It's better this way. Talking means giving away facts I need to suppress. It's logical. It's right, and yet, I am so ultra-aware of Liam beside me that I can barely taste the few bites of food I force down. Any woman—heck, any human being—would be. There's nothing more to it. He's gorgeously carved, like a fine work of art. That's all it is. Isn't it?

"You didn't tell me why you're going to Denver."

The question surprises me and my fork freezes in the rice I'd been pushing around. In sixty seconds flat, I go from relieved that he has broken the silence to panicked at the idea of sharing my new lies. I'm not ready. I don't ever want to be ready.

23

I cut him a sideways look and my pulse leaps when I find
him watching me. I'm rattled at how easily he draws a reaction
from me, and I'm almost snappy as I counter with, "Why are you
headed to Denver?" And darn it, there is a tiny quaver to my
voice I hope he doesn't hear.

"So that's how it is, is it?"

My brow furrows and I set my fork down. "What does that
mean?"

"You give what you get," he replies, and there is no
mistaking the challenge etching his words.

No, I think. That's not how it is. That's not ever how it has
been. Not in my world. "Wouldn't life be better if that's how it
truly was?" Another quaver ripples in the depths of my question. I
really need to stop talking.

This time he sets his fork down, turning to face me more
fully. "You do know that for a 'give what you get' philosophy to
work, that someone still has to give first, right?" And there is
something as intimately inappropriate to the way he looks at me,
and how he says the words, as there has been when he's touched
me.

"And you want that to be me," I state, intentionally leaving
off the question mark. I try to leave out the breathless quality of
my voice, too, and I fail. I don't like that I fail. It's another sign I
have no control over myself. Worse. I think I might like it if this
virtual stranger had control over me, which tells me how
emotionally on edge I really am.

"I'm in discussions to be part of a downtown Denver
building project," he surprises me by saying. Giving before he
"gets".

"What kind of building project?"

He just looks at me. So much for being done with friendly
banter, I think as I cave to his silent demand I "give" a part of
me. "I was laid off and my old boss got me a new job in Denver.
And before you ask, it's nothing exciting. It's administrative."

He tilts his head slightly. "So you'll be staying in Denver."

24

"For a while," I say, and the satisfaction I see in his eyes surprises and pleases me far more than it should. I ask the obvious question, telling myself it's simply because it's expected. "How long will you be in Denver?"

"It all depends on whether I take on the project." The flight attendant proves she has brilliant timing again by picking right then to take away our plates, leaving me with an incomplete answer I want completely. By the time, we've been offered coffee and dessert that we both decline, I have no idea if he would have said more, or how to get things back on topic without seeming too interested. And I am too interested. He's a risk. He could be a mere stranger or he could be an enemy. Worse. I'm too risky for anyone to befriend. I put them at risk, and with that blistering thought, I know there is nothing more to ask him. Nothing more to say but "have a nice life". I cannot ever be close to anyone. No one. Ever.

I snuggle under a blanket the flight attendant has left me, and surprising me, Liam reaches into the seat pocket in front of mine and removes what looks like a sketchpad, which I hadn't noticed until now. He pauses halfway between my seat and his own, glancing at me, and he is close, his mouth within leaning distance. It's a great mouth, sensual and full, and I wonder what it would feel like on mine.

"If you want to sleep," he says, "I promise to keep Godzilla at bay for you."

He couldn't have said anything more perfect and I know right then what it is about Liam that makes him so irresistible. Men have been scarce in my life, namely because of my fear of getting close to anyone. The few times I've broken that rule have not turned out well, and I admit that in a few lonely, weak moments, I've indulged in my share of Cinderella fantasies where my Prince Charming swoops in and makes life better. Liam is good looking, confident—he radiates control in a way my fantasy Prince Charming would. But more so, I believe Liam would fight Godzilla if he had to. Maybe not for me, but for someone he cares about.

"I'll hold you to that," I finally say, unable to find even a thread of jest to lace the words.

I watch his eyes flicker, the color diluting to a soft blue then darkening again, and I am not sure how to read the meaning when he is otherwise guarded, as much a mystery as who I am running from. "Good," he replies simply before he leans back fully into his seat.

I let my head drop to the cushion, and for a few minutes, I indulge in a fantasy about Liam to keep the monsters of my past at bay. But as the hum of the engine starts working me over again, flickering images of the past begin to slip inside my head, and I start to unravel. I'm not going to be able to sit here without getting lost in my own head and going crazy. A flash of flames has me jerking to a sitting position and my hands go to my face, my elbows to my knees. I can feel the heaviness of Liam's attention. He's looking at me but I don't want to look at him. If I do, I will talk to him. I will ask him questions. He will ask me questions.

"Amy?"

His voice slides through me, and somehow it manages to be soothing, warm comfort and sensual fire at the same time. Not for the first time, I'm baffled by the way a man I barely know manages to be silk on my raw nerves, but I'm not going to overanalyze it. I have to hold myself together until I'm someplace safe enough to cave to a little temporary weakness, and he feels like the answer. He's what will get me through this flight. I sit back to look at him, and though I'm perfectly aware that he is a heavy dose of delicious man, my heart still races as his dark good looks and his piercing blue eyes into view.

He sets his pencil down on his tray and abandons his work for me, giving me a concerned assessment. "Everything okay?" he asks, and I think of him as a gentle lion in that moment, only it is me who is purring under his powerful male attention.

"Fine," I reply, because "fine" is nothing but a word. There is no agreement on my end, no lie. I tilt my head back. Liam closes his tray and does the same, sticking his pad beside his seat.

With both our heads on our cushions, for several seconds we stare at each other and for moments I am lost in the deep blue pools of his eyes. "You do know," he says slowly, "that as a man I've been taught that a woman never means 'fine' when she says 'fine', right?"

I might have smiled another day, but not this one. "I guess we all have our own ways of defining fine."

He studies me a moment, then another, and I have the impression he's trying to understand me. I want to tell him "good luck". I don't even understand me. "You don't want to sleep."

Somehow, I don't openly react to the surprising change of subject and too accurate of an observation. Dodge and weave, I tell myself. Dodge and weave. "I don't like to sleep in public places."

"Talk to me, Amy," he murmurs softly.

"Talk to you?" I ask. I want to talk to him. That's the problem.

"You need to fill the empty space in your head, and right now, talking is your only method of doing that."

I try to joke away his suggestion. "And you'd rather talk to a stranger than have her fall asleep and get you in trouble with the flight attendant again?"

"We aren't strangers anymore, and I find the idea of occupying your time increasingly appealing." His eyes light. "So use me, baby."

The air crackles between us and there is no denying the growing attraction I have for this man. "Fine, then. I'd love to hear about the project you're traveling to Denver to discuss."

"There isn't a lot to tell yet. It's a typical property development deal. A group of deep pockets get together and aspire for greatness that equates to dollar signs in their eyes. In this case, it's a plan to create the world's largest event center, complete with concert facilities, a shopping mall, and an office complex."

He sounds blasé when I'm excited just hearing about the project, and I find I'm more curious about Liam than ever—enough to be nosy. "Are you one of those deep pockets?"

"There are too many egos fighting in one room for me on this one. Egos translate to delays and problems."

He didn't deny he has deep pockets. I was right. He is money, sex, and power. "So then, what's your role, if not investor?"

"I'm the architect they want to design the project."

I sit up straighter at this surprising news. "You're an architect?"

"Yes."

"An architect that could create a project of the magnitude you just described?"

"Yes."

"Would I know any of your work?"

"I've done a few high-profile projects."

I frown. "Isn't this where you drop names and impress me?"

"Do I need to impress you?"

My cheeks heat. "No. I…most people…"

"I'm not most people."

No. No, he most definitely is not most people. "Have you thought about your design for this project?"

"I've drafted my vision, but I already know it's not likely to please the financiers."

"But they requested you. They must like your work."

"They want me to create the tallest building in the United States."

I blink. "Could you really create something of that magnitude?"

"'Can I' isn't the question. 'Will I' is the question. Height is a short man's dream of perfection. It's also narrow-minded. How high you stand isn't as important as how magnificent you are."

Magnificent. The word resonates deeply for me. I'd once thought I'd be a part of something I could describe that way. I'd like in some small way to be a part of what he describes that way. "Are you allowed to show me your design?"

"I'm allowed to do whatever the hell I want." He reaches for his sketchpad and thumbs through it to open to a particular drawing, and starts to hand it to me, but pulls back. "I don't normally show my work to anyone until it's complete."

"But you're going to show me?"

"Yes, Amy. I'm going to show you."

He offers me the pad and I accept it, but my attention remains on him. "Why would you show me what you show no one else?"

"Because I want to."

I do not know what to say. "I…thank you." Touched and confused, my gaze lowers to look at the drawing and shock radiates through me, trapping air in my lungs. I blink, certain I am not seeing what I am seeing, but the image remains the same. He showed me what he shows no one else, and what he has shown me is a piece of my past. Adrenaline courses through me. That can mean only one thing. I shove the pad beside me and reach for his right arm and turn his wrist face up, searching for the tattoo that would tell me if he's my handler.

Chapter Four

His wrist is bare and I grab the other one, afraid my memory of which arm the tattoo was on was wrong. But there is nothing. No tattoo. No proof he is a part of my past or my future. My eyes lift to his and he arches a brow. "Problem?"

"You don't have a tattoo?"

His lips quirk and his eyes light with mischief and heat. "Not that I can show you while we're still on the plane."

I ignore the inference that he will show me later and focus on searching for what lies beneath his amusement, but I find nothing. No secrets. No hidden agenda. But then, if he expected my reaction to the drawing, why would he react any other way? Then again, I could simply be losing my mind. I drop his hand that I am boldly holding and grab the sketchpad again, staring at the drawing of a high rise framed by a pyramid. It's just a pyramid. There's not a code in the center. It's not tall and narrow like the one on my note. It really doesn't resemble the tattoo at all. Maybe it really is just a building design. Maybe it has nothing to do with me or my father at all.

Liam leans in close to me, his arm brushing mine and sending a jolt of awareness through me. "My design inspiration came from the two years I spent in Egypt, working with a team of experts that studied the Great Pyramid."

Impossibly, my skeletons have jumped out of the closet and attacked me and him in the process, and he's not even questioning what must have seemed to be my bizarre actions. Confused, I turn to look at him. "You aren't going to ask why I just...did what I did?"

"No. I'm not going to ask."

"Why?" Why would he not ask if he didn't know why I freaked out?

"You'll tell me when you're ready."

"I'm not going to be ready before this plane lands."

"That's fine." He lifts a chin at the sketchpad. "You still haven't said what you think of my vision."

He's confusing me. Okay, everything is confusing me, but his question is an escape from explaining myself and I take it. "The design is what you said you wanted it to be. It's magnificent."

"You aren't even looking at it."

"No. I'm looking at you. The man who created it." The man who wanted me to see what he wouldn't show anyone else.

"And what do you see looking at me, Amy?"

"What you let me see."

He looks intrigued by that answer, maybe even pleased. "Ask me what I see when I look at you."

More than I want him to. "No. I don't want to know what you see." I turn away from him, sinking low in my seat and pulling the blanket to my chin, and I am clear on only one thing. I don't like who I've become.

***

"Wake up, Amy." I blink at the feel of a hand on my shoulder and turn quickly to find Liam leaning over me, his mouth impossibly close to mine.

"I was asleep again?"

"Like a rock."

"Please tell me I didn't scream."

"No. Nothing like that. We're about to—" The wheels hit the runway with a hard bump and I am shocked to realize that I've not only slept a second time, but so deeply that I had no idea we were even hearing the landing announcements. It's like my mind had just shut down.

"I didn't want the landing to scare you," Liam explains, settling back in his seat.

"Thank you. It would have." I sit up, adjusting my skirt and folding the blanket.

"What's your plan from here?"

"Plan?"

"Do you have a ride to wherever you're going?"

"A friend is picking me up," I croak out, and the lie is like wet cotton in my throat. He wants this…this whatever we started to continue and so do I, but I can't know his real motivation any more than I can risk his safety by being seen with him.

"Male or female?"

I blink, snapping back to the present. "What? Male or female?"

"Your friend picking you up. Male or female?"

I know the safe answer is "male". I know that if his motivation for the question is simple male interest, it will discourage him, and still I hear myself say, "Female."

His eyes darken, heat, and I think he's pleased with my answer. "I'll help you with your bags."

"No, I—"

"I'm helping you with your bags, Amy."

There is command in his voice, and I am instantly, unbelievably aroused, and pleased at his insistence, when I should be running for the hills. I will run for the hills when the doors open. "Thank you," I murmur and turn away from him, afraid he will read my intentions to flee. Quickly, I make sure my folder and bag are intact, sliding the leather strap over my shoulder, and I am ready for action.

The plane parks at the gate, and Liam stretches his long, perfect body to retrieve my bag from the overhead compartment. Once he hands it to me, I lift the handle and tell myself to make my escape, but for a moment, I am frozen in regret over leaving him. Too soon, he jerks his bag free, and I am out of time. A man moves between myself and Liam and I take the opportunity to dart for the exit. I don't look back. I want to look back.

A few minutes later, I am outside in a cab line that stretches a good fifteen cab lengths long, with no actual cars in sight. Thanks to several conventions and some Hollywood event, it appears I have plenty of time to savor my regret over leaving Liam behind. And I do. I savor it like I would water in a desert.

I'm busying contemplating how good he might have tasted when a black Town Car stops directly beside me. The door opens and to my shock, Liam steps out and grabs my bag. "Come with me," he orders, and he doesn't give me time to argue.

I haven't moved yet and he's already at the trunk where the driver lifts my bag to deposit it inside. I consider leaving it behind and running. I should leave it and run. I charge toward him and meet him at the back door.

My chin lifts and he is taller than I realized, and his sleek goatee is impossibly sexy, nearly distracting me from my anger. "You can't just take my bag and demand I come with you."

"And yet that's exactly what I did. Get in the car, Amy."

I bristle at the command. "I don't know you."

His piercing blue eyes darken. "I have every intention of remedying that."

A thrill shoots through me at the obvious promise that he will be my lover, and there is no denying that I am seduced by this man, drawn to his confidence and dark good looks. To the gentle lion I believe will take control of everything around him, including me. The man who will demand much of me, and perhaps take more than I should give. And yet, beyond all reason, I want to experience those things. I want to experience him. It almost feels…necessary.

A cab honks at our driver and I have nothing to go on but instinct that tells me I can trust him, but it has never failed me. Not even when I took the job at the museum that I knew was a mistake. The horn blasts again and I go with my gut. I get in the car. Liam follows me inside and shuts the door.

"Where are we going?" the driver calls over his shoulder, pulling away from the curb.

I quickly slide my bag from my lap to the seat in between Liam and me, and I'm suddenly too nervous to look at him. He's experienced in ways I can't even pretend to be, in ways the few men I have dared to date have not been. Worldly in ways I once thought I'd be. And with the folder I've been given by my handler opened, I read out my new address, trusting him at a time when trust is the last thing I should be dishing out.

"I approve," Liam says as I seal the zipper up again.

"Approve?" I ask, daring to look at him, aware of him on every level. His size. His spicy scent. The burn of his anger in the depth of his stare over my leaving him behind that hasn't quite faded.

"The location your new boss picked for you. It's a safe area."

I seize the opportunity to know more about this man I am risking so much, perhaps too much, for. "You know Denver that well?"

"Yes. I know Denver quite well."

"Did you design another building here?"

"The tallest one downtown."

"I thought you weren't into the whole 'bigger is better' thing?"

"It was a notch on the proverbial bedpost of a young architect."

I can't help but wonder if I'm setting myself up to be a notch on his proverbial bedpost as well. "You're still young."

"I started young, so I seem younger than one would think a seasoned architect might be."

"When you say started young that means what?"

"I was an apprentice to a very famous architect from the time I was thirteen until he died four years ago."

"Thirteen? You started your career at thirteen?"

"I started my training at thirteen." He lowers his voice. "You do know I couldn't let you run, don't you?"

"I wasn't—"

"You were."

"If you think that, then why'd you come after me?"

34

"Because you didn't want to run. You just thought you had to."

"That's a little arrogant."

"It's honest. I like honesty."

I like it too, but I can't give it to him. This ride was a mistake. "Liam—"

He closes the distance between us, moving my bag out of the way, his powerful leg pressed to mine, his fingers sliding into my hair. I am shocked. I am excited and scared, frozen and burning up at the same time. "Do you know how much I like it when you say my name?" he asks, his voice a soft, seductive purr.

Nerves and heat collide like fire in my belly. He likes when I say his name. This man who is overwhelmingly male, a powerful force like none I have ever experienced. "I don't know what to say to that." And it is as honest an answer as I've given anyone in years.

"You don't have to know, Amy. It's okay not to know."

For the second time today, he has spoken words straight to my soul. Relief that reaches so far beyond this moment in time, and my possible response to his statement, flows through me. This is why I'm in this car, why I am drawn to this man. He makes me feel I don't have to hold the world up on my own. And as crazy as it is, from the moment my eyes met his in the terminal, he has had a way of making me feel I am not alone.

His thumb runs over my bottom lip and a shiver trickles down my spine. I think he will kiss me. I want him to kiss me. But he doesn't. "Soon," he promises, as if responding to my silent plea, as if he knows how much I crave his mouth on mine. His cell phone rings, but for a moment he ignores it to add, "And not soon enough."

He moves away from me and I want to pull him back. I want to feel his hands on my body again, his leg pressed to mine. But he is already answering his call, and too easily dismissing what I cannot. "Yes," he says to his caller. "I'm here."

My fingers curl, nails digging into my palm. I have no one to call and ask if I'm here. I have only me and no matter how drawn

I am to Liam, if today has proven anything to me it's that there can always be only me. But as I glance at Liam's strong profile, I pretend he is truly with me. And that I am truly with him. It is a small dream in the middle of a nightmare.

***

Thirty minutes after we leave the airport, the Town Car pulls to a stop at a destination. Liam grabs my bag and exits street side while the driver opens my door. I step outside, enjoying a cool evening breeze that drives home the fact that I am no longer in New York. Scanning my surroundings, I appear to be standing in the center of high-end restaurants and stores where, despite the late hour of nearly midnight Mountain Time, people are casually strolling the sidewalks and the city is far from dead.

With my apartment key in my hand, I glance behind me to find more stores and a hotel, and then forward again where apartment balconies seem to sit above the retail stores.

"Hang onto my bags," I hear Liam tell the driver, before he joins me, my joke of a suitcase and my bag in tow. "What apartment number?"

"222, but I don't see an entrance."

"The driver said there's an elevator entrance beside the kitchen store."

Spotting the "Sur Le Table" sign he must be talking about, I turn to Liam and reach for my suitcase. "Thanks for the ride."

He holds on to both of my bags. "You're alone in a new city. I'm not letting you go inside an apartment you've never seen before by yourself."

"The driver—"

"Has been tipped well." He motions me forward and starts walking, effectively giving me no room to argue.

Staring after him, I am on unsteady ground, inexperienced with a man as dominant and stubborn as this one. I didn't think this part of the evening through when I accepted the ride. I have no idea what awaits me at the apartment. What if there is something I can't let Liam see?

Double stepping in my high heels and not all that gracefully, I catch up to him. "You really don't have to—"

He cuts me a sideways look. "Right. I don't have to. You don't have to. But we are, baby, and we both know it."

My heart sputters at the obviously naughty sexual reference. "I was talking about walking me to the door. You don't have to walk me to the door."

He shoots me an evil smile. "I wasn't."

"Liam—"

"Amy." We stop at an elevator and he punches the button, amusement dancing in his eyes. "When do you start work?"

The elevator dings and opens. "I don't know." I dart inside the car, trying to think of an answer that isn't a lie.

He steps in beside me and punches the button. "You don't know?"

"I'm supposed to get settled first."

He scowls, and even his scowl is handsome. "How well do you know your new employer?"

Now I scowl. "How well does anyone know their employer?"

"You moved here for this person."

"A job is not a person, and I know just as much about him as I do you." The elevator opens again and I don't give him time for a rebuttal. I step into a carpeted hallway that reminds me of a hotel corridor and note the sign pointing me to my right.

"Your boss didn't make sure you got here safely tonight," he points out as he joins me, and we make our way to the last apartment at the end of the hallway. "I did. Do you have your key?"

I hold it up between two fingers and stop in front of the assigned door. I just can't think of it as "my door". "I'm all set."

"I'm coming in to make sure you're safe."

"This is good," I assure him quickly.

"You have no idea what waits on you inside."

37

Exactly. "An empty apartment and I don't know you, Liam. I can't invite you inside." And I have no idea what makes me say it, but I add, "Not tonight."

"That's better than not ever," he comments. "But I'm not a serial killer and for all I know, your new boss is. Let me check the place out for you. You can stay outside while I do."

"I'm not letting you in."

He leans in close and presses his hand on the door above me. I can feel the heat rushing off his body. And as silly as it seems, I can't explain it, but I can almost taste the masculine scent of him. Or maybe I just want to taste him. "I'm going to get a room across the street," he informs me.

"Your hotel is across the street?"

"It is now. I'll be back in fifteen minutes with a list of restaurants open at this time of the night we can choose from. My name is Liam Stone, Amy. Look me up on your computer. Then you'll know I'm trustworthy."

"I don't have a computer."

"Or enough clothes to be moving from state to state."

I left myself wide open for that one. "I had them shipped along with my computer."

He doesn't look convinced. "Right. Of course. Look me up. Use your cell phone."

"It's broken. I have to get a new one tomorrow."

"It's broken." His tone is flat.

"Yes. It's broken."

He considers me a moment. "Stay here and don't go inside yet." Without further explanation, he walks toward the elevator.

Confused, I open my mouth to call after him and snap it shut. It's midnight. People are sleeping. He steps into the elevator and regardless of what he's planning, I know he'll be back, which means I need to act fast. I unlock the door, flip on the light and tug my suitcase and bag along with me.

A small hallway leads past a kitchen to my left and directly into a large open-concept dining and living area. Thankfully, I do have furniture, which is more than I had when I was sent to New

38

York. I scan and quickly dismiss the overstuffed brown couch and two chairs. It's the envelope sitting on a simple wooden dining table that has my attention. I set my bag down and sink into one of four chairs, reaching for the envelope. The contents I find inside are disappointingly uninformative. There is only a lease to the apartment with a note telling me to sign it and drop it by a real estate agent's office. The first month's rent is paid. Nothing else. Absolutely nothing. No information about what has happened. No words to explain the threat I might be under. No triangle symbol. It's not there. My heart starts to race. There is supposed to be a symbol on any instructions I get. I don't know what this means. Maybe he thought this note was an extension of the last so it didn't need it? I can't think. I have to get rid of Liam and go to a bank machine and see how much money I have to live on. Should I run? I don't know. I just don't know. I have to take one thing at a time. Liam first. The rest later.

Shoving away from the table, I rush back to the door, and open it, gasping when I find Liam standing there, dark blue t-shirt stretched over his impressive chest, and he doesn't look happy. "I told you not to go inside. It wasn't safe."

If having him, or anyone for that matter, worry about me didn't feel so good I might have bristled at his reprimand. "Well," I say, "as you see, I did go inside, and I'm happy to report that Godzilla is nowhere in sight."

He does not look any more pleased than moments before. "We'll talk about that later."

My brows dip. I'm not sure I'm processing all content properly right now. Why wasn't the symbol on the note? "Talk about what?"

"Later," he repeats tightly, and hands me an iPad. "My Wikipedia page is up. Look it over. There's a hotel directly across the street. I'll get a room and suggestions for places to eat that will still be open."

My eyes go wide. "You have a Wiki page?"

"Yes. I have a Wiki page, and despite the unauthorized information it contains, it's fairly accurate. I'm going to check into my hotel. I'll be back to get you in a few." He starts to turn away.

"Liam, wait." He pauses and looks at me. "You do know that I don't have a Wiki page. I'm not a model or an actress or a celebrity of any kind. I'm not even a secret heiress to a mega-fortune."

"You're you. That's what counts." He turns away again and I don't stop him.

You're you, he'd said. Only that's the whole problem. I'm not me.

Chapter Five

R ich, sexy, and powerful no longer seems an adequate description. Liam Stone is, per Wikipedia, a reclusive billionaire and philanthropist who lost both of his parents at a young age and was taken in by one of the most famous architects who ever lived. Liam inherited his mentor's extreme wealth and apparently, his skill. At the young age of thirty-one (apparently most architects are older when, and if, they become established) Liam is the highest-paid living architect, and is considered an architectural prodigy.

Setting the iPad aside, I press my fingers to my throbbing temples. It's almost comical that I actually thought Liam could be my handler. He has far more to occupy himself with than little ol' me, and I really don't know why he's hovering around me at this point. Well, except maybe he just wants to have sex. I'm not above admitting it's on my mind. Heck, maybe I should just embrace a potential one-night stand and let Liam take me away for a few hours. Whatever awaits me tomorrow will still await me tomorrow. It might even stop me from melting down. So why do I feel so let down that this thing with him isn't more? I can't have more. There is no "more" for me. I went to the door to get rid of him. When he comes back I should pretend I'm not here.

A knock sounds and I discard the idea of not seeing Liam again, jumping to my feet and rushing past the kitchen. Afraid I might talk sense into myself, I waste no time opening the door, and then almost swallow my tongue with the impact Liam Stone has on me standing there. He might be a billionaire, able to afford the finest of fine, but the man does a pair of faded Levi's and a t-shirt as right as they can be done. And he does it while looking at me like I'm the dinner and he's going to lick me off the plate.

"Done with your research?" he queries.

"Yes. I read your Wiki page."

"And?"

"You're rich, talented, and why are you at my door again?" And why am I not sending you away?

"Because you haven't invited me in yet."

"You sure don't seem like a recluse to me."

His lips quirk and he straightens, and before I can blink, he's advanced on me, his hands coming down on my shoulders, his big body crowding into the apartment. "Liam," I object. Sort of. Actually, I'm not sure I object at all.

"Amy," he counters.

My nerves prickle. "Don't do that."

He kicks the door shut, pressing me against the wall, his powerful thighs encasing mine. "Do what, baby?"

The endearment does funny things to my stomach and so does the solid wall of his chest beneath my fingers. "Mock me when I say your name."

"Ah, now, little Amy, I assure you I am not mocking you. I already told you how hot it makes me when you say my name."

I am so not skilled at this flirtatious word game he is playing, so I resort to what I do well. "I didn't invite you in."

"No?" he asks, his eyes alight with sexy amusement.

"No," I reply and while I am nervous, out of my league with a man this experienced, this incredibly sexy, his playfulness somehow takes the edge off.

"Yes, well," he says, his voice holding a hint of evil mischief, "I prefer privacy when I kiss you. We recluses are like that."

My nerves shoot to the sky. Kiss me. He wants to kiss me. I want him to kiss me. "You're no recluse," I accuse, wondering how the Wiki got that so very wrong.

His eyes darken and narrow. "Then how would you describe me, Amy?" he asks, his voice low, gravelly. Affected. By me. The idea is exciting and frightening all at once.

"Demanding," I say, and I sound as breathless as I feel.

His fingers curve around my neck, tugging my mouth near his, teasing me with the promise of a kiss. "You have no idea just how demanding I can be." And with that erotic promise, his tongue slices into my mouth, a silky, hot caress that seems to touch every inch of my now tingling body. The taste of him, of hot passion and desire, sizzles through my senses, and my fingers splay on the hard wall of his chest.

A low groan escapes his throat and his hand caresses over my hip and palms my backside, pulling my hip flush with his, his thick erection pressing into my belly. "I've wanted to taste you since the moment I saw you in the terminal," he murmurs, and his breath is warm, a wicked seduction against my mouth.

"Feel free to do it again," I whisper, and I am surprised at the boldness of my words. But then, I've never had anyone as tantalizingly male as Liam Stone to inspire me.

"I'm going to do a whole lot more than kiss you, baby," he promises, and his mouth covers mine, his tongue once again pressing past my lips, and I feel the lick between my thighs, in the deep throb of my sex. I have never wanted like this and I like it far too much to let inexperience, or a note on a bathroom mirror, interfere. This is one night for me. One night. Where that concept had bothered me before, it feels remarkably liberating now.

My nerves have nothing on my desire to lose myself in this amazing man, who is like no one I have ever known, who I will probably never see again. Determined to enjoy every minute with him, and every inch of him while I'm at it, I sink into the kiss, my tongue caressing his, drinking him in. Boldly, I slip my hands under his shirt, my palms flattening on hard muscle beneath warm, taut skin. Touching him is wonderful, addictive. I am trembling inside, aroused in a way no man has ever made me feel.

Confidence builds inside me and my hand strokes a path down his zipper. His hand goes to mine and he tears his mouth

LISA RENEE JONES

from mine, his fingers move from my neck, tangling in my hair, tugging me backwards with a gentle, erotic force. "How old are you?"

The questions shatters a little part of me not even fully realized. This is not a reaction a girl wants when touching a man. "Why does that matter?"

"How old, Amy?"

"Twenty-four." I don't even know why I answer. I shouldn't have answered.

"How many men have you fucked?"

I gasp. "You can't ask me that."

"I just did. How many?"

I don't like where this has gone. I don't like how I suddenly don't know if he thinks I'm a virgin for my limited experience or a hussy for my fast actions. Either way, this is not an escape anymore. I try to shove away from him, but his grip in my hair doesn't loosen. "Let go," I hiss. "This was a mistake. I don't know you. I don't do this kind of thing." Great. Now he thinks I'm a virgin. I can't get this right. "I mean, I do. No. I don't. I don't do this kind of thing."

"It's quite clear you do not do this kind of thing," he says, releasing me, and I hate how much I wish he had not, after what he has made me feel. Or how relieved I am when he plants his hands by my head, caging me as if he doesn't want me to escape. "But I do, Amy. I do this kind of thing. I have short, quick, well-protected affairs with women who get that I'm not going to be around tomorrow. Women who do not care enough about who I am to find out my name or how much money I have."

My defenses flare, verging on anger. What is he accusing me of? Being a virgin, a slut, or a money-grubber? "I didn't try to find out about you. You made me read the Wiki page. You made me."

"I know. I wanted you to know me and to trust me. I still do."

I soften, confused. I stay confused with this man. "I don't understand. You just said…and I know and…why are you, and I

44

and…" My God, I'm an educated woman and I've lost the ability to form coherent sentences.

"The same reason I showed you my design on the plane."

"Which is why?"

"Because against every rule I have ever set, I wanted to."

"I don't know what that means."

"Then let me be more clear." His cheek slides over mine, his whiskers scraping erotically over my delicate skin, his lips pressing to my ear. "You're a beautiful woman who deserves to be properly fucked, which I conclude from both your actions and answers to my questions, that you have not been. I want to be the man to remedy that. I want it very much." His arm wraps my waist, shackling me to him as if he fears I will get away, his free hand stroking down my hair, as he huskily adds, "Probably too much." He moves then, his intense blue eyes staring down at me, searching my eyes. "I don't know what you're running from, but I know you're running."

My heart jackhammers. "No, I'm not. I'm not."

He brushes his lips over mine. "And I'm not asking you to tell me why," he says, rejecting my denial. "But just know that I have every intention of making you forget everything but what it feels like to have my tongue and my cock buried inside you."

My lashes lower and heat pools low in my belly, then settles hard between my thighs. I've never even had a man use the word "fuck" with me before, let alone promise to fuck me properly, but I fear he will make me forget why my silence is golden. "I don't—"

"Look at me, Amy." There is a command in his voice and for reasons I cannot explain, I am compelled to comply. My gaze lifts to his. "I do," he promises. "And I like the idea that I am the man who'll make sure you do, too."

He'll make sure I know. This is exactly everything I need to hear. He's promised to be demanding and to take me to unknown territory, but that I won't be there in the dark. I am so very tired of being in the dark. I wrap my arms around his neck and make sure he knows how important this is to me. "I want to know. I need to know."

Approval seeps into his eyes, heat simmering in their depths, and one of his strong hands cradles my face, and then his mouth is lowering to mine. His tongue licks into mine, tasting me, and he is different now, we are different now. The kiss is hotter, wilder, passion unleashed, and I have a sense of being claimed. Like I am his to take and I want to be taken by this man. I want it very much.

Still kissing me, as if he too cannot get enough of me as I cannot of him, he lifts me off the ground, his hands cradling my backside. My legs wrap around his waist, and one of my shoes falls to the ground, so I kick the other one free. "Where's the bedroom?" he asks, a gravelly urgency to his voice that mirrors what I feel.

"I don't know. The right, I think." I sound urgent. I am urgent.

He starts walking and I bury my head in his neck, inhaling his scent, and tiny splinters of memory begin to pierce the fog of desire. I shove them away, refusing to be consumed by the past when I have this man to do it for me.

I resolve to lose myself in kissing every inch of Liam's neck, but as soon as I make a move, he curses under his breath. I struggled to see behind me. "What? What is it?"

"No sheets, pillows, or blankets," he informs me, and he's already retraced his steps until we've re-entered the hallway. "Your boss should have made sure this was handled."

"I'm sure he didn't think—"

"Exactly," he concludes. "I'm taking you to my hotel, where I can lick you from head to toe on proper bedding."

"What? Liam. No." He shifts my weight and reaches for the door. "Stop!"

He straightens and he does not look pleased. "Stop why?"

My mind races for an answer, for one of the many lies I live to tell. "My apartment is directly across from the hotel. I'll see the staff around the neighborhood. I don't want them thinking of me as the floozy some rich guy brought to his bed for a night every time I walk by."

He arches a brow. "Rich guy? Floozy?"

"That's what it will seem like, Liam."

He scowls and lowers me to the ground, pressing me against the door, his hands settling possessively on my waist. "You aren't a floozy. You know that, right?"

I hate the excuse I've made, the lie that is my life, and the idea that it might push him out the door, that he might not ever touch me again, is unbearable enough to give me courage. "If you want to fuck me, it's here and now. Otherwise, goodnight, Liam. Thanks for the ride."

He leans back and rests his hands on his hips, no longer touching me, and I am shaken by how much the loss of the connection with him affects me. I am used to being alone. I am used to not being touched. "This is crazy, Amy. Your apartment isn't ready to be lived in."

My apartment. This place is not and never will be my apartment. It isn't mine. It will never be mine but he can never know that. "I need to stay here tonight," I say, and I am not pleased with the way my voice cracks.

Liam notices, too. I see it in the slight flicker of his eyes. "You need to be here?"

"Yes." And my voice is no stronger now than moments before, damn it. "I need to be here."

He leans in, one hand on the wall by my face his big body close but still not touching me. Why do I need him to touch me this badly? "Then I need to be here tonight," he declares. "We will be here tonight."

We. I know the word really means nothing. This is a night. That's what I want. He's made it clear that is what he wants. But I like the idea of being "we" right now. And I desperately want to get back to forgetting everything but him. I push to my toes and press my lips to his.

His arm wraps my waist again and he pulls me close, his body a warm, welcome shelter from the nightmare I've left

47

outside this door. "I'm not going anywhere you aren't tonight," he promises.

Tonight. It's enough. It has to be enough. It will be enough. "Good. I don't want you to."

I've barely said the words, when he turns me to face the door. "What are you doing?" I demand, catching my weight on the door with my palms.

He steps closer, his hips framing mine, the thick ridge of his erection pressed to my backside. "Preparing you."

"Preparing me?" I gasp. "What does that mean?"

He tugs my jacket down my shoulders and I expect him to pull it free, but instead he tangles it around my arms and turns me around to face him. "You can free your hands, but don't."

"No. No." I knew he'd ask for too much. I knew. "I can't do this. I can't—"

He cups my cheeks. "Deep breath, baby. I know you're on unfamiliar ground and I know you barely know me, but I'm just going to make you come. Pure pleasure, nothing more. I know when things feel out of control you think you need control. But sometimes, having a safe place to give it away is the best way to block everything else out. I'm asking you to let me show you I'm that safe place."

But he'll be gone tomorrow and where will I be? What place will my mind have traveled, and will I get back to where I was before? "Do you ever give away control?"

"No. That's not what works for me."

"But you think it will work for me." It's not a question. It's clear what he thinks. I just want...more. More understanding. More...him.

"It will work for you. Let me teach you, Amy."

Teach me. This is what he'd been talking about on the plane and this is so far into new territory, I don't know which direction to go. I crave what he will show me but I fear what I will show him.

"Do you have things you need to block out, Liam?" I ask, and I am on tenterhooks, waiting on an answer that feels important to me, when I do not even know what I expect—or want—it to be.

"Yeah, baby," he surprises me by saying, "I do. Knowing you need the escape and admitting it, if only to yourself, is control." I am shocked by his admission, by his willingness to share something so personal with me. I am beyond aroused by this man and when his finger traces the skin at the top of my blouse, I feel the touch in every part of my body. "I did." He starts unbuttoning my blouse. "And now I'm going to show you how we escape together."

Together. I like how that sounds, but...

"Right here in the hallway?" I ask, and my blouse begins to gape, exposing the thin lace covering my breasts.

"Right here in the hallway," he agrees, his hot gaze raking the swell of my breasts, his deft fingers finishing the buttons and quickly popping open the front clasp of my bra. He covers my breasts with his hands, and nuzzles my neck at the same time, and the mix of erotic and tender ignites my senses and soothes my nerves. "You smell like sunflowers."

"My perfume," I whisper, and unbidden, my mind my goes to New York, to my apartment where it, and everything else I own, and no longer have, are located.

"It's perfect," he approves, tugging my nipples, and the unexpected, bittersweet ache leaves room for none of the burn for what is behind me. There is only the burn for now, for him, for the escape he has promised me. My lashes flutter and just that quickly he is on his knees, inching my skirt upward, and there is only the emptiness that is my ache to feel him inside me. I am in a haze of desire, and my skirt is somehow at my waist, his tongue tracing the top of one of my thigh-highs, then traveling up and down my leg. The urge to tug my hands free, to tunnel my finger into his thick, dark hair, and force his mouth where I want it, is almost too much to bear.

"I want to touch you," I pant. "I need to touch you."

His eyes meet mine, and they are hot with desire and dark with command. "Not yet," he orders, and with no warning, he wraps his fingers around the thin strips at my hips and tugs my panties down to my feet. I step out of them. Or I think I do. I don't know. Everything is a haze of nerves, and desire, and need. But they are gone and Liam's fingers are exploring the slick, wet center of my body, and his mouth is on my upper thigh, teasing me with where it might go, where it hasn't gone and I soon hope it will be.

He slips two fingers deep inside me and there are panting, moaning sounds filling the air that I barely recognize as coming from me, and I try to control myself, but I cannot. I'm not sure I'm really trying. I am so wet and so aroused, I am certain I will come ridiculously quickly. The idea is embarrassing and I try to will my body to calm. I try to resist the pleasure building low in my belly and spiraling into my sex, but it is growing, consuming me like a black hole where nothing but pleasure exists. It reaches out to me and drags me deep into the center of spiraling, delicious sensations. They overcome me, he overcomes me, and my sex clenches so intensely that I jerk and my knees go weak.

Liam's arms wrap around my lower body, holding me up and his tongue laps at me, fast and hard and then slowing as I soften, as my muscles ease, and I relax. He tears my jacket from my wrists and I wrap my arms around him for stability and bury my face in his neck. He drags me with him, until he is sitting against the door and I am straddling him and all I can think is how embarrassed I am. How long did I last? One minute? Two? Please let it have been at least five.

"Amy," he murmurs. "Look at me."

"No. I can't."

"You can," he says firmly, and his hand goes to my head, tilting my face to his. "Don't be embarrassed."

Now I'm embarrassed that I am embarrassed. "I can't help it." My voice shakes. I'm not sure it's just my voice. I have never felt this exposed. Not since…not ever. Not like this. "I was—"

"Beautiful." His hand moves to cup my cheek. "Absolutely beautiful and sexy."

My hand covers his. "No." I laugh and it's a choked, horrible sound. "I was fast. Really embarrassingly fast."

"I like that I can turn you on that easily." He caresses my shirt and bra from my shoulders, and I let them fall away and my mind is mush all over again. And when he leans in and tenderly kisses my shoulder, his hot stare raking over my naked torso, my breasts are instantly heavy, and my nipples tight. "And I like," he adds, his eyes lifting to mine, "that you like it when I look at you." His finger lightly teases my nipple and a shiver of pure pleasure slides down my back. His lips curve. "And that you react when I touch you."

A pinching sensation begins to form in my chest. I'm overwhelmed emotionally when I should simply be aroused and nothing more. I barely know this man and somehow he digs deep into my soul and speaks to me like no one else ever has. It's today's events. It's not him.

I cut my gaze, trying to pull myself together, but he does not allow me an escape, not one he has not created, or offered in perfect orgasmic pleasure. His finger slides under my chin, tilts it up, forcing my eyes back to his. "Don't hide what you feel. See, baby, that's the thing about fucking properly, it's raw and honest. There's no time limit, or embarrassment, or nerves, which should exist. It's just us fucking. Us feeling. Us being us together. We leave everything else at the door." He smiles a sexy, easy smile and his hands slide up my back, his forehead resting against mine. "Well. In our case, on the other side of the door. Don't ever be embarrassed with me."

My fingers curl on his cheek, the soft rasp of his newly formed whispers teasing my skin, the tension of moments before fading into the seduction promise of his words. "I'm trying. This is…" My voice trails off, and I am uncertain what I was going to say, uncertain what I really feel.

"I'll help you." He drags a finger down my cheek. "The only reason I wanted to go next door was that I want this to be good for you. And I think you need to be pampered tonight."

51

"I can't," I whisper, and the two words, so telling, so honest, are out before I can stop them.

He leans back and I am naked beyond my blouse, exposed beneath his too-keen inspection. And I think he can see what I heard in my voice. My desire to escape into his world and run from mine, if only for a little while. My fear for him if I were to do so. My fear now that I have let him see too much.

Steeling myself for whatever questions he will ask, I wait for him to break the silence, hating that my passionate escape with this man will now be washed in the lies the rest of my life is drowning in. But there is only silence, and in that silence, understanding. He seems to know where he can push me and where he cannot, and I do not understand how a man who was a complete stranger yesterday knows me this well today.

Holding my stare, he reaches behind him and tugs his shirt over his head, and the anticipation of seeing him naked, of being naked with him, drums wildly through my body, but that moment doesn't come. Immediately, he puts his shirt over my head, the spicy scent of his cologne teasing my nostrils, mingling with my confusion. "What are you doing?" I ask, reluctantly shoving my arms through the sleeves.

"Making sure you know I'm here to stay. I'll be here with you tonight. I'll be here with you in the morning. And you'll still be wearing my shirt because we both know you have no clothes in your suitcase."

Chapter Six

I shove away from Liam and push to my feet. "I told you, my things are being delivered."

He's already standing in front of me, towering over me, distractingly bare-chested except for the perfect sprinkle of dark hair over his pecs. "I'm not asking for answers," he assures me. "Explain it to me when you're ready."

It? Explain it? "When I'm ready?" Does he not understand I will never be ready?

"When you're ready," he repeats, removing his cell phone from his pocket. "I'm going to have the hotel deliver sheets and pillows."

"No. I didn't invite you to stay. You were only helping me in the door."

"Are you saying you don't want me to stay?"

"You were supposed to help me in the door," I repeat.

"As I remember it, I did."

"Liam—"

"You want me to stay."

"That's arrogant."

"It's honest."

Honest. I wish he would stop using that word. "You can't stay."

"Do you want me to stay?"

Now it's a question. And yes. Yes. I want him to stay. I should say "no". The word won't leave my mouth. "It's not that simple."

He reaches for my hand and pulls me close, and I tell myself to push away but I don't even try. "Let me make it simple, Amy. You want me to stay. I want to stay. I'm staying." He strokes my hair. "And you need help. I'm going to help you, baby. You aren't alone."

A tornado of emotions rolls through me, and the debris of my past is like glass cutting me inside out. Becoming his charity case is so far from being Cinderella it's like a horror show, not a fairy tale. I'll take alone any day. "No." I hiss out the word, and this time it comes from my mouth. "I don't want your help."

"You need my help."

I'm emboldened in my mix of anger and mortification. "How did we go from you fucking me properly to me being the needy girl you met on the plane you want to help?"

"Correction. The gorgeous woman I met on a plane and still plan to fuck properly many times over if I have my way. And there's someone who needs help in my path every day, and yes, I help where I can, but Amy, I'm here, with you, because you are you."

"Stop saying that," I blurt. "You don't even know who I am."

"But I want to."

And that's the problem. I want him to and he can't. "One night. We were making this one night."

"Were we, now?" He arches a brow and looks amused. "I don't remember that agreement, so I'd better start making my case for two. Starting with making tonight good for you."

Good for me? Does he not think a world-shattering orgasm was good for me? Surprising me, he pulls out his cell phone and starts to dial. "Who are you calling at this hour?" I ask, suddenly worried. Has a Wiki page given me a façade of safety with Liam I shouldn't trust? I don't know this man and he knows too much about me.

"This is Liam Stone," he informs the person on the other end of the line, amusement lingering in his eyes. "I checked into the presidential suite about thirty minutes ago. Yes. Right. Everything is fine, but I'm at a friend's apartment across the street and one of her moving boxes is missing. She needs queen-sized sheets, pillows, a blanket, towels, and toiletries. I'll pay double whatever your listed price is to have them brought across the street to me, and whoever delivers the items will be well rewarded."

I press my hand to my face and turn away from him, walking to the end of the hallway to stare at the apartment that is not mine, but is all I have. What have I done by bringing Liam here? He's determined to help me now and I can't tell him who I am, but he has money to uncover whatever he wants to uncover. Lots of money. If my handler doesn't have my bases well covered, Liam will find out who I am. It could get him and me both killed.

"Perfect," I hear Liam say, and I can tell he's moved closer. "And just to be clear," he continues, "I have the suite indefinitely, if you could make sure that's on record."

Indefinitely. The idea that I might be across the street from this man, and I can simply ignore him, is pure insanity. You don't have to be a rocket scientist to know that you don't just ignore Liam Stone if he doesn't want to be ignored.

I turn back around to find him closer than I thought, with only a few steps separating us at the most, and I look away, knowing I'm not quite as collected as I need to be. In the process, my gaze lands on his flat, naked stomach. My mouth goes instantly dry and not just because of his lack of clothing, which would be enough in itself, but it seems I've found Liam's hinted-at tattoo. The number 3.14 is etched in his skin over the Pi mathematical symbol, which frames his belly button. Beneath the symbol are rows of numbers I know represent infinite value, all aligned as an inverted triangle, and trailing downward to alluringly disappear into his pants.

"What options do we have for food at this hour?" Liam asks the hotel operator, or whomever he is talking to, and the sound of

55

his voice snaps my gaze upward. His eyes meet mine, and now his amusement is laced with male satisfaction. He leans on the edge of the wooden dining room table and holds the phone away from his mouth. "Is pizza okay and if so, what kind?"

Pizza, not Pi, Amy. Keep your gaze up and stop thinking about where those infinite numbers stop. "Cheese. I like cheese." I dart past him and head to the kitchen, needing space, needing to think.

Once I'm behind the wall of the tiny, rectangular cracker box of a room, I wish I could take a jog. Running has been my salvation over the years, a way I found to block out the things that mess with my head. Instead, I just try to do anything I can to stay busy. I open cabinets to see if I have any supplies. The answer is no. No supplies, nothing to organize or clean. No place but Liam to put my mind and he's no longer an escape. He's just trouble.

Pressing my hands to the counter, I let my head fall between my shoulders. I have nothing but the clothes I have on my back—or actually, that now lay on the hallway floor—and there is a billionaire standing a few feet away. The irony is hard to miss.

Liam's voice lifts, growing closer again, and it is deep and confident, from a man who owns his world when I do not own mine. I think maybe he owns it more than I do right now, and that is a sign I need that run and some time alone. I am weak tonight, but I will claw my way back to strength again. I will. I have no choice.

I listen as he orders two large pizzas, one cheese and one pepperoni, and remembers my diet Sprite from the plane, which I am far too pleased about. The man is impossibly, frighteningly, involved in my world in all of one day. My crappy college boyfriend I'd gambled on, thinking he was my age, and far removed from my past and therefore safe, sure hadn't known much about me. I'd thought that was good, another thing that made him safe, until I found my roommate's legs around his neck.

"Food and supplies should be here in about fifteen minutes."

I turn to find Liam standing under the archway of the kitchen entry, his dark hair rumpled, his broad and gloriously bare chest reminding me that I'm wearing his shirt. And while he is strikingly male, that is not what steals my breath in this moment. It's the mix of tenderness and heat I find in his eyes.

"You didn't have to do that," I whisper.

"We both need to eat."

"That's not what I mean, though I appreciate the food. You didn't have to order the hotel to bring me things. That costs money, and—"

He advances on me and I swallow the rest of my sentence. I start to back away but he is already in front of me, his hands on my waist. I suck in a breath, and just that fast, I'm on the counter, skirt up, knees apart, and the fingers of one of his hands tunnel into my hair. His mouth slants over mine, his tongue licking into my mouth, and he doesn't taste tender. Not one little bit. He tastes like the raw, honest passion he's promised this night will hold. And he tastes like me. It is a sultry, arousing thought. I sink deeper into the kiss, and this time, I am the one tangling my fingers into his dark hair.

He reaches for my hand, covering it with his, tearing his mouth from mine. "I told you I do not do anything because I have to. And I don't. But to be inside you right now, baby, I have to. I need to. And, yes—right here in the kitchen." He pulls his shirt over my head and I don't know where he tosses it. I am already wrapping my arms around him, pressing my naked breasts to his chest. He strokes a hand down my hair, brushing his lips over mine. "This isn't going to be proper, but I'll make it up to you, I promise. If I don't find my way inside you now I won't let you eat when the food arrives."

"The only thing you'll have to make up to me is if someone comes to the door before this happens."

"They'll wait if they have to," he promises. "Put your hands on the counter behind your back."

"What?"

"Do it, Amy. Let me look at you."

The inherent shyness life has taught me freezes me, and Liam seems to know immediately, but he is not discouraged. He presses my hands and molds them to the counter behind me with his own. "Leave them there."

I don't speak. I am so nervous and aroused. He brushes his lips over mine. "Say 'yes', Amy."

"Yes," I whisper, and he smiles.

"You really are so damn sexy."

"I don't feel sexy right now."

"Then what do you feel?"

"Out of my league." And it is a relief to actually say what I really feel.

"If anyone is out of their league, baby, it's me. You're an angel and I'm...not." He glances up at the ceiling, as if he's struggling with something, before his stormy gaze returns to mine. "Maybe that's the appeal for both of us. We're different, dark and light. Right and wrong. Now, don't move or I'll show you just how not an angel I am."

The threat is darkly erotic, arousing, but it does not stop me from seeing pain and self-loathing deep beneath his surface that I relate to far too well. I want to know what made him, what drives him, what haunts him in the night, and I don't care what he says. Something haunts him. And I want to be the angel he sees me as, when I know that I left that "me" in the past.

I will never be an angel to anyone but him, and that will be a one-night façade. "I won't move my hands, Liam. Not if you don't want me to."

I watch his eyes dilate, darken, his jaw tightening into a hard line, and this is not the reaction I had hoped for. His hands move from mine to rest on my shoulders. "Now I'm going to fuck you, Amy." There is a new gruffness to his tone, and I almost feel as if he's trying to shock me, to prove that I'm the angel, and he is not. But then he drags his fingers downward, trailing over my breasts to caress my nipples. His touch is light, teasingly gentle, and when it is gone, I gasp with the deep ache in my sex, where I want him to be. "I don't like the way you won't let me touch you."

"You can touch me." He unzips his pants and shoves them down, his hard cock jutting forward, thickly veined, and reaches in his pocket and pulls out his wallet. "Later."

I only have tonight. I only have tonight. "Promise me," I insist, and for reasons I do not try to understand, I need his agreement. "I need you to promise me, Liam." And my voice is raspy, filled with emotion that reaches beyond touching him. I want more and I don't even know what "more" is.

He sets his wallet on the counter, a wrapped condom now in his hand, and presses his palms to my knees. "I promise, Amy." He leans in and kisses me, his mouth lingering on mine a moment, as if he is savoring me, and I feel the connection to this man in some deep part of my soul. I can't explain it. Maybe I just need to create this in my mind to survive the day or justify what I am doing. But it is right for me now. He is right for me now.

Slowly, he leans back, and it is as if a simmering fire sparks back into life. His gaze holds mine as he tears open the condom and discards the wrapper. My heart thunders in my ears and my sex aches with the emptiness in me that only he can fill. He looks down to roll the condom on, and I cannot help but think about how prepared he is, how normal this is for him. I do not have time for my mind to go crazy. He is quick and in seconds, his mouth is back on mine, and each delicious swipe of his tongue seduces me more. He is a drug that delivers passion and escape.

He tears his mouth away, watching me as he curves a hand under my backside and lifts me. His gaze lowers, raking over my breasts, heating my skin, and then his free hand wraps his cock and he slides it along the sensitive lips of my sex, back and forth, until I question how urgent he truly is, and I am panting with anticipation.

"Please, Liam," I whisper, far less shy now that I am desperate to feel him inside me.

The instant I issue the plea, he reacts as if that was what he was waiting for. He presses inside me and drives deep, filling me, stretching me, and now both of his hands cup my backside, arching my hips just how he wants them. He sinks in, burying

59

himself to the deepest part of my body, and pleasure slides over his features. "Oh yeah, baby. You feel like heaven." He lowers his head and licks one of my nipples, then suckles, and the sensation spirals through me, straight to my lower belly. My sex clenches around him, and my hips arch.

"Liam," I pant, needing what he still hasn't given me, needing him to move.

His lips taste mine. "Say my name again."

"Liam," I whisper, and I wonder why this appeals to him. What it means or if it means anything at all.

"What do you want?" he asks, and his voice is gravelly, laden with desire. Desire for me.

"You know what I want."

"Tell me." He reaches between us and strokes my clit.

"You know what I want." My voice is louder now, laced with the urgency building inside me, and I wrap my legs around his hips, touching him the only way I can touch him.

"Say it, Amy. It's just you and me. Raw and honest. Give it to me."

Honest. That freedom is everything to me. "Fuck me. I want you to fuck me."

A look of pure male satisfaction rolls over his face, and he slides his hands around my back. "Hold on to my neck," he commands. The instant I comply, he lifts me, melding my body to his, and he starts to pump, pulling me down on top of him at the same time. Pleasure nearly overwhelms me as each thrust of his cock sends shock waves of pleasure through my body. I do not know if I am actually on the counter or he's just using it to brace our bodies, or his knees, I think, but I don't care. I bury my head in his chest, and cling to him, the sound of his heavy breathing like silk stroking my nerve endings. I can feel his urgency, his need, and I am there with him, pushing into him, trying to meet him, take him, find that sweet spot that we both want. And it's there, it's there, and the sexy near growl that escapes his lips tells me it's there for him, too. He grinds me against him, and my sex clenches around his cock, and I am shaking, or he is shaking.

Maybe we both are. It's a haze of pleasure rushing through my body, and I am clutching him and he me, and I feel the counter beneath me, his arms around my back.

"That's what you call fast," he murmurs against my neck, kissing it and my ear before leaning back to search my face. "What are you doing to me, woman? I'm never…" He scrubs his jaw, seeming almost rattled, before his hands go to the counter at my hips. "Next time won't be like that. Slow, baby. Nice and slow."

Next time. I am pleased with these words and stunned at the idea that I have affected this man on a level beyond his normal encounters. I surprise myself by smiling. "I didn't even get to examine the many attributes of Pi."

His lips curve. "Baby, you can examine it, lick it, do whatever you want to do to it and me, after I feed you. I promised. I meant it."

Lick it. Yes. Please. Promise. I am not used to promises. I will take this one and put it to good use. He pulls out of me and I gasp. "Warning, please."

He laughs, a gentle lion's laugh, deep and sensual. I love that laugh. "We have to get you dressed before someone shows up at the door." He sets me on the ground and eyes the condom and motions to the other room. "I'll be right back." He heads out of the kitchen, probably to the bathroom, and I suddenly realize I don't even have basics like toilet paper. Now this is truly embarrassing. I'll have to find a twenty-four-hour store and get some basic stuff. That's all there is to it.

I wiggle my skirt down my hips, and snatch up his shirt, but I don't put it on. Liam will need it to answer the door. His words play in my mind. Be inside you now. I have to. I smile to myself at the idea of making a man like Liam "have" to do anything, and I hunt down my panties, bra, and blouse—which appears to be missing a middle button. Nothing like a gaping front to show off your bra. Heading to the living room, I can hear Liam talking to someone on the phone from the bedroom, telling them how to find the entrance to the building. Knowing we will have company soon, I quickly shove my clothes into my carry-on bag and pull out the airport t-shirt I bought before leaving New York.

"The bellman is coming up the elevator now," Liam says, rounding the doorway just as I pull the t-shirt into place. Stopping dead in his tracks, his expression turns suddenly stormy and intense.

Feeling more than a little awkward at his reaction, I hold up his shirt. "I thought you might need this and I tore the button off of my blouse."

He stalks forward and stops directly in front of me. "I have never hated an 'I love New York' t-shirt more than the one you have on."

His voice is a tightly pulled cord. He's angry and I'm baffled. "You hate 'I love New York' shirts?"

"I hate what it says about your situation." A knock sounds on the door, but he doesn't move. Silence ticks between us and I think he has to be able to hear the thunder of my heart. Another knock and he turns away, pulling his shirt over his head as he stomps toward the door.

I wet my dry lips and stare down at the shirt, and I feel like an ice pick is chipping away at my nerve endings. I hate what this shirt says about my life, too. And I hate that Liam knows what it says about my life. I hate it because it means I have to make tonight our only night. I knew that already, but I also know a part of me was slipping into a fantasyland where I could allow Liam to be my Prince Charming for just a little bit longer. I'm back now, though. I'm back in reality and no matter what happens tonight, I won't forget that it translates to one thing and one thing only. Alone.

Chapter Seven

$$\pi$$

L iam has done his best to convert my apartment into his penthouse suite for me.

I wait by what is supposed to be my new kitchen table where two pizzas fresh from the hotel kitchen wait on us, and listen as Liam sees two hotel staff members out the front door, no doubt tipping them well. In all of fifteen minutes since their arrival I have everything I would have had, had I been in Liam's room: bedding and pillows, as well as enough paper products, plastic utensils, kitchen items, and basic hygiene products to last me days. The list goes on, with a hair dryer, hotel slippers, and a robe, and my kitchen is stocked with canned sodas and a coffee pot with supplies, including cups. I am truly doubting my decision to stay here rather than go to his room, and not just because he's likely spent a pretty penny on me. Because I am surely the talk of the hotel now and Liam is exposed by his connection to me.

Dragging a hand through his thick, dark hair, looking tired but incredibly sexy, Liam walks back into the room. "The pizza smells good."

"Yes," I agree, but my mind is elsewhere and I hold my hands out to indicate the apartment. "Liam, this, all of this you did, is too much."

"It isn't even close to too much."

"It had to have cost you a small fortune."

"I have a fortune, Amy." And he sounds almost…bitter? About being rich? He grabs the pizza boxes that are stacked with a couple of sodas and plasticware, and motions to the bedroom. "Let's go eat on the bed."

Dinner in bed with the sexiest man I've ever known. I don't have it in me to complain. "Yes. Okay, but thank you for everything. Thank you so very much."

"It's not your thanks I want."

"Then what do you want?" And I don't know why, but I hold my breath, waiting for his answer.

He tilts his head and studies me a moment. "For you to share dinner in bed with me."

I let the air trickle from my lips. It is the perfect answer, even if I sense it wasn't what he really wanted to say. "I'd like that."

I excuse myself to go to the bathroom and quickly change into some shorts I purchased when I bought my t-shirt, and while doing so, I begin to worry dinner is an opening for Liam to drill me with questions. But I don't let myself linger in the bathroom, where I'm dodging the mirror. I won't like what I see in it.

Reassuring myself that I'm good at dodging what I don't want known, I join Liam on the bed. With my legs curled to my side, and the pizza boxes on the mattress between us, I dig into a slice of pizza with a hunger, not for food, but for something no one can take from me. My love of cheese pizza is like every little personal part of me that no name or location change can strip away.

"Why don't I tell you about your neighborhood?" Liam suggests, dusting off his hands, after digging into his food with a heartiness that beats mine by double.

"You know it well enough to tell me about it?"

"Actually, yes. I consulted on a building project not far from here a few years back. I stayed across the street for a month. When you come out of the building, go right a block and then left, and there are two coffee shops and several restaurants. If you go left instead of right when you exit, two blocks down in a straight line is a mall. There's a Whole Foods to the right of the mall and another grocery store to the left. You have everything from doctors to hair salons all in a small radius. A lot like New

York. Which is good, since the city as a whole is not. Most people have cars, and I assume you don't have one of those being delivered tomorrow."

My heart sinks at what I haven't considered, and I fight the urge to set down my half-eaten second slice of pizza, afraid I will give away how rattled I am. Instead, I pause on a bite and say, "No. No car," before chomping down on more than my food. I now have one more thing I haven't thought about and will have to face tomorrow.

"You do have your personal belongings being delivered, right?"

On that question, I abandon eating, setting down my slice and reaching for my soda, effectively avoiding eye contact with Liam. "Yes. I'll have my things tomorrow." It's not a lie, I tell myself. Whatever I buy will be here.

He shuts the lid to his pizza box and I set down my drink and do the same with mine. I'm not hungry. That's the thing about lies or almost lies. They make everything else harder to swallow along with them. I wonder if that is why he ignored the second half of his pizza. He can't swallow it with my lies either. And now he's just staring at me. He's good at that, I've discovered, really darn good at fixing me in his bright blue stare and seeming to see right through to my soul. I almost think his silence is as dangerous as his questions. He's analytical, a smart, calculated thinker. I see it in his eyes, and his job and his success backs up my assessment. I have to get him to stop trying to piece together my story.

I scoot to the headboard, pull my knees to my chest, and work for diversion. "You don't seem like a recluse."

"Subject of your belongings diverted," he comments. "Check. That's one of the 'when you're ready' topics." Blood rushes to my cheeks but he doesn't give me time to reply, continuing, "I learned privacy from Alex, who was my mentor. He lost his wife and child in a car accident a year before I met him."

"Oh God. How old was the child?"

He moves the pizza boxes to the floor and then sits against the headboard beside me, and we both turn to rest on one shoulder to face each other. "I never saw a picture. Looking back, I think seeing her hurt too much."

And I wish for a picture every day of those I've lost, and it terrifies me that I can no longer remember their faces. It terrifies me that Liam is so near, so able to read what I feel. It terrifies me that he won't be tomorrow. "To lose a child must be the worst kind of pain."

His lips draw into a grim line. "I'm told it changed him, though I have no comparison. I didn't know him before he lost them. He didn't talk about them and he didn't do press or make public appearances. When I began getting my prodigy architect buzz, he told me the hype could go to my head and ruin me, thus forbidding me any press as well. I deviated from his no-press policy one time, and one time only, when he was still alive. It was a hard lesson I've never forgotten. My ego and desire to share my success with the world was at Alex's expense. His personal story ended up in the papers. He went crazy on me and then crumbled like I didn't think he could crumble. That day changed me forever. I forgot about my ego and to this day I rarely grant interviews and I rarely do appearances."

A little part of me softens for Liam, and I don't know what overcomes me. I reach up and touch his jaw. "Now I know why you're so tight-lipped about your accomplishments."

He grabs my hand and I am somehow more complete because he's touching me. "I keep my private life private and I let my work speak for me elsewhere."

I want to tell him how much I envy his confidence and sense of identity that he doesn't appear to need anyone else to validate. But if I do, he'll ask me about who I am and who I want to be and even if I could freely talk, I couldn't tell him what I no longer know. "That still doesn't spell recluse to me."

"That started a couple of years ago when a particular reporter hounded me about an interview. When I wouldn't give it, she wrote a scathing piece about me."

His thumb begins stroking my palm and heat is radiating up my arm and seems to have set my vocal cords on fire. "Scathing?" I choke out.

"It read pretty much like 'he's rich, talented, and good-looking, but the man is a recluse with the social skills of an ant.'"

I gape. "An ant? No, she didn't?"

"I assure you, she did."

My lips curve and I fight my laughter, and lose. He leans in and brushes his lips over mine. "You think that's funny, huh?"

I curl my hand on his jaw and I am charmed at how easily he shares his story, how wonderful it is to talk to someone, to touch someone. To touch him. "I don't mean to laugh."

"It just happened."

I nod. "Yes, but not at you. That description is so over the top it's comical. And it's not you."

"Not me," he repeats, his hand sliding to my hip. "Are you sure about that?"

I've spent my whole adult life reading people, sizing them up, weighing them by degree of potential threat, and I've trusted him from the moment I first found myself captured by his presence in the terminal. "Yes," I confirm without hesitation. "Yes. I'm sure." The air shifts around us, crackling with electricity, and I am empowered by how comfortable I feel with him despite my situation and the disparity of my experience to his. "You are rich, talented, and good- looking, but I forgive you all of those things because you're charming and funny."

His eyes shadow, turbulence waving through the heat. "You were right earlier," he says, and he pulls me close, molding our bodies together, his hands spread wide on my back.

My hand lands on the hard wall of his chest and his heart thunders beneath my palm, telling me he is calm and cool on the outside, but I've hit a nerve and I don't know why. "Right about what?"

"When you said that I let you see—but Amy, I see more than you want me to see."

But not more than I wish he could see. "Then stop trying."

"That's not going to happen." He brushes his lips over mine, his tongue licking into my mouth in a slow, seductive caress. "We've already gone too far to turn back."

My hand is on his cheek, my legs intimately entwined with his, neither of which I remember doing. "Yes," I whisper. "We've gone too far, Liam."

"And yet not far enough," he replies, stroking the hair from my eyes, his voice rough sandpaper and masculine heat.

The intensity of what I feel in this moment and for this man hits me like an earthquake exploding from somewhere deep inside, a deep, dark crevice of my soul. My emotions are all over the place. I do not know where this man is taking me, and I am as desperate to find out as I am to stop him. The need to run and hide or stay and fight is equally intense. He must read this in me because he softly orders, "Turn out the light, Amy."

Turn out the light. I do not question his command. I act on my need for self-preservation, and I turn over and flip out the lamp on the nightstand, relieved at the sanctuary that is the darkness. Even more so in the sanctuary that is Liam's arms as he pulls my back against his chest, his hand splaying possessively on my stomach. My lashes lower and I relax into him. I do not know how this man is both the refuge I run to and the reality I am running from, but in this moment, that is exactly what he is to me.

His hot breath fans my neck and his lips brush my ear, the delicate touch sending a shiver down my spine. I expect him to kiss me again. To touch me and to fuck me, as he's vowed. I want him. I even need him tonight and I inhale, savoring the now-familiar spicy male scent of him, and this time there is no memory splintering through my mind. There is just the darkness I hide inside, the soft bed, and the hard man holding me.

***

I blink into the light and don't move, trying to process where I am and what is happening. An unfamiliar closet door becomes the first focal point I manage to identify and my brain processes where I am. New apartment. Denver. Liam. I jerk to a sitting position, searching the room to find he is nowhere to be seen. My heart twists in several painful knots. He's gone. I glance at the digital bedside clock the hotel brought me last night and note the time of eleven o'clock. Of course he's gone. I was one of his many flings and he has work to do. How have I slept this late? How did I sleep at all in my state of mind, and without any nightmares?

I'll keep Godzilla at bay, Liam had said on the plane. It had been the truth. He had. Somehow, some way, this stranger had given me enough peace to get through the night. And while I should be freaked out that I didn't hear him leave, I'm pretty sure my mind used Liam as we had used each other for sex. For an escape. He had given me something else to focus on instead of my situation, and clearly allowed me to shut down mentally and hold myself together. Liam had been an unexpected gift. Who was gone.

Standing up, I ignore the gut-wrenching feeling of being alone. I've done this for years. There's no reason I can't do it now. Besides, I was never alone or my handler wouldn't have known when I was in trouble, but where the idea of his existence has comforted me in the past, it doesn't work this time. I can't go through this again. I have to have an exit strategy of my own. One that gets me off everyone's radar, including my handler.

I walk to the living room to assess the rest of the apartment in the daylight and my breath hitches as I spot a package sitting on the kitchen table with a note. I reach for the wall to steady myself, an icy chill sliding through me at what this means. My handler has a key to the apartment.

Chapter Eight

$$\pi$$

The air feels thicker, my breathing more labored, and I barely remember walking to the table. I am simply there, staring down at what has been left for me. The box is white with an Apple logo on the top, and this does not seem like good news to me. Is the new phone I received last night, and haven't used, already compromised in some way? Am I moving again? Is this location unsafe? My adrenaline spikes and I grab the small white envelope and pull the card from inside out.

> Amy -
>
> It's not safe to be without a phone. This is yours to keep and the service is paid for a full year. And don't say "no" when I'm not there to argue the many reasons you have to say "yes". Think about your safety and convenience. Besides, I selfishly do not want to wait to hear your voice until I see you again. My number is programmed in the phone. Text me when you get this and I'll call you at a break from my meeting.
>
> Liam

A sense of relief washes through me and I become aware of my free hand balled at my chest, where my heart is beating like a drum. I inhale and will it to slow. I'm okay. Everything is okay. The note isn't from my handler. I am not leaving another city. I am not running. I am only hiding. Or maybe I am running. I don't know how to define what I am or what I do anymore, and suddenly I am exhausted when I've only just woken up.

I sit down and touch Liam's signature, blocking out everything else. He didn't walk out the door today without saying goodbye. He doesn't intend to say goodbye at all. I'm blown away that he took the time before heading to his meeting to go out and buy me a phone. No one has done anything like this for me since I was still living at home. Home. The word, the place, the past, crashes over me. Sometimes I dream of throwing away fear and returning. Sometimes I think that facing the danger rather than running from it is my better option. But how do you face what you do not fully know?

My gaze falls on Liam's neat, masculine script and my lashes lower. For a few moments, I let myself indulge in the memories of Liam's velvety, warm kisses and sensual caresses. I remember the "pi" tattoo and the numbers that formed a triangle that disappeared deliciously below his belt line. I remember his husky voice when he'd said, "Baby, you can examine it, lick it, do whatever you want to do to it and me, after I feed you. I promised. I meant it." A shiver of pure desire tracks down my spine, but my eyes land on the envelope with my lease inside and it's like a knife has cut open the sultry veil of fantasy I'm hiding beneath. My handler wasn't here today, but he could have a key. I wonder if he'd had a key to my first place in New York. I shiver again, and this time it is not with desire. I am creeped out in a big way, and I'm having my locks changed.

I shake myself and stand up, setting the note from Liam back on the table, uncomfortably aware of my circumstances. Liam is a distraction and a problem I cannot afford. No matter how much I might want to see him again, I cannot. I won't. Sleeping through the sound of a feather dropping isn't an option to me, let alone relaxing with a man I barely know to the extent I sleep through the opening and shutting of doors. Liam was good for one night, a bridge to the next day in the face of a crisis. I'm on the other side. I hope.

***

Thirty minutes later, I've showered, and I'm looking ridiculous in my new t-shirt and a skirt, with high heels I intend to replace quickly, but the t-shirt seems better than a gaping blouse. To add to my disorderly appearance, I stare at the light blonde poofball that is my hair in the absence of a styling product and a flat iron, and decide I look like I just stuck my finger in a light socket. I am what my mother would have called a "hot mess", and I try to hear her voice in my head and fail, which is why I normally don't try. Failing hurts.

Giving up on my appearance, I snatch my small purse and head to the kitchen table, and put all my new cards and ID in my wallet. Gathering my lease and the cell phone I intend to return to Liam, I decide I need to take my now empty carry-on with me. I load it up with my purse, paperwork, and the phone. I'll be dropping it by Liam's hotel sooner than later to avoid any chance of running into him. And thanks to the to-do list I wrote and rewrote about five times before I dried my hair, I head to the door feeling a tad more in control than when I woke up. Lists do that for me. I write things out when I need structure. I rewrite them when I still don't feel I have it all pulled together. Or I clean and organize. Or I write lists in between cleaning and organizing. Maybe that should be my cover. I'll be a maid. No one would expect to find my father's daughter cleaning up after other people, and it would control my stress. It isn't my dream career, or what I went to school for, but I have to find a way to get back to where I was before the museum, where surviving was more important than dreaming.

I step into the hallway outside the apartment (I'm not ready to call it "my apartment") and I'm locking up when I hear the door directly behind me open and shut. I turn and jolt to find myself locked in the penetrating stare of a man as tall and devastatingly male as Liam, but that is about where the comparison stops. While Liam has a worldly, refined, and somehow edgy air about him, this man is a rugged bad boy from his torn, faded jeans to his long, light brown hair tied at his nape.

"New to the neighborhood?" he asks, shifting a leather backpack to one of his impressively broad shoulders, and my gaze falls and finds his Dallas Cowboys t-shirt, and the link it represents to what was once my home momentarily knocks my breath away.

"You okay?" he asks, and my gaze jerks to his. Was I obviously rattled? I'm never obviously rattled. "You look like you saw a ghost."

"Yes," I say quickly, silently warning myself this could be a trap, a way to lure me into admitting some connection to a past I cannot claim. "I'm new to the neighborhood. I just moved in last night."

His gaze flickers over my clothing and lingers on my t-shirt, the way my gaze had on his. "Just a hunch," he comments, "but moving here from New York?"

"Yes," I confirm, hugging myself, embarrassed by the reminder that I am a frizzy, mismatched mess, "and unfortunately, my clothes didn't make it from the airport." I sound nervous. I am nervous, and I only wish I had the luxury to let it be about his good looks, not his intentions. But I do not. "My outfit is certainly a way to make an impression."

"I've lost a few bags in my time," he says, and his words are as warm as the interest I see his eyes. He's warm and oddly familiar in some way that I cannot identify, but it doesn't make me uneasy. In fact, it's comfortable. "And," he adds, his voice a little softer, "I don't think you need a t-shirt to make an impression." He motions to the elevators. "I'll ride down with you." He starts walking.

I stare after him, trying to dissect what he meant. I don't need a t-shirt to make an impression. Is that good or bad? Bad. It's bad. No matter the reason, I don't need to be leaving impressions of any sort on anyone. Double stepping, I hurry behind him to catch up and again remind myself of what time has taught me. Bad hair and funny clothes bring attention just like being overtly sexy does. I have to fade into the background, play mousy librarian like I have in the past. Or clean houses, or whatever it might be. I've lost the library as a cover. Anything I once did I can no longer do.

We stop at the elevator and he punches the button. "I'm Jared Ryan."

"Amy," I provide, and force myself to say more and embrace this new identity in a believable way. "Amy Bensen. Nice to meet you. You live in the apartment across from me?"

"For a month or so," he says, but doesn't offer more. I want him to offer more. "What brings you to Denver?"

I have no idea why, but I feel like a deer in headlights. The doors to the elevator open and I rush inside, tired of spinning tales. "I hear there's a great mall right up the road," I reply as he joins me inside. "That's all a girl needs."

He steps into the car, tilting his head and studying me. I punch the button to the elevator and the doors shut instantly. He keys in the floor. "You moved here for a mall you've never checked out?"

So much for familiar being comfortable. "It's been a long time." It's not a lie. Never is a long time. A very long time. "How far away is it?"

"Cross at the stoplight and you'll be at the mall."

I don't like how keenly he is looking at me. Like Liam, he sees too much and I think his one-month stay is probably a good thing. The doors slide open and I don't waste any time escaping to the walkway outside, a high wind lifting my hair around my shoulders.

Jared joins me and motions down the sidewalk. "Just walk straight and you will run right into the mall."

"Thanks. Nice to meet you. I'm sure I'll be seeing you again."

He steps a bit closer. Really close, actually, and I can smell his cologne. It's warm like the man, and it reminds me of Texas cedar on a spring day. He glances downward, his gaze landing on my feet, and he inspects my open-toed shoes and my pink painted toes for so long, blood rushes to my cheeks. Over my feet. That's a new one.

His attention lifts, eyes narrowing almost suspiciously. "Are you walking in those shoes?"

"It's close. I'll be fine."

"You want a ride?"

Yes. No. Yes. No. No. No. Not only does Jared see too much, he has this easiness about him that would make running my mouth far too easy. "I appreciate the offer, but I'd like to go explore my new neighborhood."

He considers my reply for a moment, his lashes lowering, and then lifting. "I'd offer to show you around, but I have a meeting."

It could be a polite comment without meaning, but there is something in his eyes that tell me it's not. I believe he would take me and show me around and I would gobble up the opportunity to talk about my old home state, or really, to just talk about anything. If things were different. If I were really Amy Bensen.

"We're neighbors." Dang it, I sound hoarse, almost emotional, not casual and friendly. What is wrong with me? "I'm sure we'll see each other."

"I'm sure we will," he agrees, and there is a rasp to his voice that carries a hidden meaning beyond the obvious. I search his eyes and I think…I think he feels this familiar comfortable thing I feel, too.

I lift my hand in a parting gesture. "See you soon," I reply, and somehow I make myself turn and start walking, but my steps are heavy and slow, my body like lead, weariness seeping into my bones. I can feel Jared's stare, and I can feel him willing me to turn back around. And I want to. I want to with a desperateness I can barely contain. The museum has given me a taste of what "normal" feels like, what friendship feels like, and I miss Chloe already. And I miss the tiny window of time when I walked around corners without fearing what was on the other side.

I pass two stores and I swear I can still feel Jared watching me. Why would he still be watching me? The hair on my nape prickles and I start to think about Jared's "Texas" shirt and the way he'd questioned me about not knowing the area. He's familiar. Why is he familiar? I don't know. I am suddenly glad I didn't cave and ask about the shirt, and that I didn't answer his questions with any more detail.

At the corner, I stop by a bank, and I rotate to face the door, pausing before entering the building to look for Jared, but he is nowhere obvious. A funny, knotted sensation tightens in my belly and it's not comfortable at all. In fact, it's downright uncomfortable, which is crazy. I have every reason to be relieved that he is gone, and as I enter the building, the cash machine appearing to my left, I have every reason to focus on what's important. Like answering the question of how much cash I have to survive.

I pull my wallet from my purse and pull out the card I'd used during my life in New York and stare down at it. The desire to claim my cash from the bank and know I have it is powerful, but out of the blue, an image of Liam comes to my mind. He's a billionaire, a man who has the money to find out anything he wants to know about just about anyone, including me. How do I know that whoever is chasing me doesn't have just as much money? What if my cards are all flagged or tracked in some way? I sigh with painful resignation and slip my card back into my wallet. If I touch that money, it has to be on my way out of town, or maybe the country. My gut says I should keep my cash card and my old identification that lets me withdraw larger amounts in my purse, just in case.

Removing the new card my handler has given me, I slide it into the machine and punch in the code I've been given, searching for my balance. My name comes up on the account and I wonder how my handler managed to set up the account without my signature. My balance is $5000. My new rent is $2200, but it's paid for this month already. I have no idea if I really will get more money as promised, and I'm too cautious to assume I will. That means I have to hold onto two months' rent to feel secure until I see another cash deposit in this account. That leaves me with $800 to buy clothes and food. I'll need more money to survive. Please let there be more money.

My head begins to spin and I remind myself my handler said he'd deposit weekly installments into this account, but when? On what day? Do I have utility bills to consider? I remove the card and head into the lobby. There is no way I'm letting anyone, not even my handler, track me by my card number. I'm withdrawing all the money now.

***

Fifteen minutes later, I'm in a dressing room in a store by the mall, wearing a pair of black shorts and a pink tank top, with a cheap, but cute, pair of black Coliseum-style sandals on my feet. And what a relief they are. In only a few blocks my feet are blistered—or, as my father used to say, my dogs are barking. I'm going to take the tags to the cash register and wear my clothes out of the store.

I'm just gathering together several other small items, enough to make three cost-effective outfits that I can wash and rotate, when the phone in my bag starts ringing. I sit down on the wooden bench against the wall and listen to it, fighting the urge to pull it from the bag. I should have taken the phone by the hotel first, but the idea of walking into that fancy place with my t-shirt and skirt on was too much. And now it's ringing and it can be only one person. Liam. Liam is calling me and I want to answer.

Without a conscious decision to do so, I reach in my bag and pull out the box holding the phone. It stops ringing and starts back up almost instantly. I set the box down on the seat and stare at it like it's some kind of alien. It stops ringing again and my stomach twists and turns like rope in a tangled mess. I'm a tangled mess. A beeping sound comes next. A message. Liam has left a message and I don't even think. As if I want to prove I am indeed a mess, I snatch up the box and open it, punching the message line and listening.

I haven't heard from you and we both know you're in some kind of trouble. Call me, Amy. Don't text. I need to know you are okay. If I don't hear from you in the next fifteen minutes I'm leaving my meeting and heading to your apartment.

A thunderstorm of emotions rushes through me, and I let the phone drop to my lap. Liam is worried about me? He's going to leave a meeting to check on me? He barely knows me. Why would he do that? We both know you're in some kind of trouble. I squeeze my eyes shut, conflicted clear to my soul. No one worries about me. No one should know enough to know to worry about me. But Liam does. He does and I want him to. I want him. The phone starts to ring again and I can barely catch my breath. I have to talk to him, and I tell myself it's not because some deep part of me craves the sound of his voice. I have to turn him away and be convincing. For him. For his safety. Money can buy things, and even people, but it can't keep him alive. Not from a threat I don't understand enough to explain.

I draw a breath and answer the call. "Hello."

"Amy," Liam says, and somehow my name is both a command and a caress.

"Liam," I reply and I like how my name sounds on his lips. I also like how his name feels on my tongue. Even more so. I like how his tongue feels against mine, how he feels when I am with him.

"You didn't text me like I told you to."

Normally I would bristle at the command, but it takes effort to muster objection. "I'm not good at taking orders, Liam."

"Is that why you didn't text me?" His voice is softer now, his tone too intimate and yet still not intimate enough to satisfy the craving his voice creates in me. I will myself to say more, to say goodbye, but I can't get the words out. I settle on, "I'm going to drop the phone by your hotel. I can't accept it."

"It's a gift."

"I pay my own way."

"The money is nothing to me and everything to you."

This time I do bristle. Money is nothing to me beyond basic survival. "Your money is nothing to me, Liam."

"And while that makes me immensely happy in some way, Amy, it does not now, when we are talking about the phone. Money is just money. You are right. But your safety is another story. You need the phone."

I think of the phone my handler gave me, and it bothers me he can track me. He can perhaps see my phone records. But won't Liam be able to do the same? "I'll get my own phone."

"Use this one until you do."

I open my mouth to object and he seems to read my thoughts. "Compromise, Amy."

Compromise. And while I feel that is all I have done my entire life, it is strangely appealing with Liam, maybe because it implies there is a relationship between us that there isn't. Is there? "I can't keep the phone."

"At least keep it and use it until we can talk about it tonight."

Tonight? "No. No there isn't a tonight. I can't see you anymore."

Silence. One beat. Two. "There is that word again," he observes, and then repeats, "We'll talk tonight, Amy."

"No, Liam. No."

"You think you're alone but you aren't."

"Because I have you now?"

"Yes. I know you don't believe that, but you will. Soon, baby, you will."

The idea of having him is bittersweet in so many ways I can't tick them off in a year. "You don't know what I think or what is important to me."

"I know enough. The rest I want to find out."

"No." But it sounds like yes. "I won't be here tonight. I have plans." Like locking myself in that cage of an apartment and going nowhere.

"I'm not going away, Amy. You do know that, don't you?"

His voice is possessive, a rasp of sandpaper over my nerve endings followed by pure silk, and it does funny things to my stomach. "I don't need a protector, Liam."

"I see things differently."

My spine locks into a steel bar. "I am not your—"

"Not yet. But I want you to be."

I blink. What? He wants me to be what?

"I'll call you when I finally get out of this meeting. It will probably be about six. One of the investors isn't flying in until later today."

I fight the urge to ask about the meeting and the investor. "Why are you doing this?" I whisper.

"You won't like my answer."

"How do you know what I like or don't like?"

"I'll see you tonight." The line goes dead and I do not know why, but I need my answer. I call back. He answers immediately. "At least I have you using the phone."

"Why are you doing this?"

"Because you are you, Amy. And I have to go, but text me if you need me." He hangs up again.

I clutch the phone. He was right. I do not like his answer. My very existence is a lie and that means anything he sees in me, anything between us, is also a lie.

Chapter Nine

After buying the clothes I had on in the dressing room and wearing them out of the store, I have to stop by the realtor's office before I go to the grocery store. The six-block walk takes me past rows of cute stores and eateries, and I find Evernight Legal Services nestled in between a coffee shop and a furniture store. I frown. I thought this was a real estate office, but it's logical enough that a law office might handle all business affairs for someone.

I head inside the office, and I am pretty much pushed through the door by a gust of wind that jangles the bells attached to the entrance. In New York, I was pushed and shoved by people. Here it's Mother Nature, and according to the store clerk I'd asked, this is normal here.

Swiping at the hair in my face, I find myself standing in a small, homey-looking, compact office, and in front of a rich mahogany desk with a narrow hallway that looks like it leads to a few offices at most. "Welcome." My gaze shifts to a gorgeous, twenty-twoish blonde bombshell wearing a hot pink dress and lipstick to match who appears in the doorway behind the desk. "Can I help you?"

"Amy Bensen." The name rolls off my tongue far easier than it had with Jared. I settle my leather bag, now packed with my shopping haul, on the waiting room chair. "I'm here to drop off my signed lease."

"Oh yes. Amy." She smiles and offers me her hand. "Luke told me you were coming by."

"Luke?"

"My boss. He's not in right now. I think he said there was a package for you."

A package? I'm not sure what to make of that. "For me? Are you sure?"

"Well, I'm new so I could be wrong, but let me go look in the mail room. I'm almost certain we had something, though." She heads down the hallway without me truly seeing her. The package has to be from my handler. It would make sense. Maybe it contains a real explanation to what is happening and why I had to leave New York, I think hopefully, and my heart begins to thunder in my chest, adrenaline pouring through me. Answers. That's all I want. It's the unknown that makes me jumpy, afraid of my own shadow.

The woman returns with a box wrapped in brown paper, reading a sticky attached. "Yep. I was right. The note says it's from Mr. Williams."

"Have you met him?" Could he be my handler?

Her brow furrows. "Dermit Williams?" I nod and she shakes her head. "No. He's out of the country. He's been Luke's client for years, I believe."

I pull the lease from my bag. "Here's the signed paperwork I was told to bring by here. I'm assuming Mr. Williams owns my building? The lease is with Evernight."

She shrugs. "I don't know, but that sounds logical. I really just started a few days ago." She offers me her hand. "I'm Meagan, by the way. You can call me Meg."

"Nice to meet you, Meg." I shake her hand. "Are you new to town or just new here?"

"New to town, just like you. I got my paralegal degree in New Mexico just this month and had a job lined up with a big firm that fell through." She holds out her hands. "So here I am."

"Oh no. I'm sorry. Why don't you go home?"

"Ex-boyfriend." She crinkles her nose. "You know. Personal drama, new life. Yada yada. Life is as perfect as a hot man in a pink hat, if you know what I mean."

I try to picture Liam in a pink hat and she is right. It's just wrong. I grin. "A pink hat on a hot man. I'm not going to forget that one anytime soon."

She grins. "I aim to make a lasting impression."

I think of Jared and my t-shirt that was so very obviously wrong with my skirt and heels. I liked him. I like Meg. As for Liam, I downright crave that man. None of this is good. None of this is staying off the radar.

"We should do coffee," Meg suggests, her voice snapping my gaze back to hers. "We're both new and all. Or drinks. There are some cool spots around here for happy hour."

"Sounds fun." And it does, but I won't be going any more than I will be calling to check on Chloe. I won't be diving into the deep, dark waters of some wild river and taking others to drown with me. I'm not that selfish and I won't let a window of weakness change that.

"You want to exchange numbers?"

"I have a new cell phone but it isn't working right. I'll call you and give you my number when I'm sure it's staying as is." I crinkle my nose. "And when I remember the number."

"I did that last week." She grabs a pen. "Let me give you my cell so you don't have to call me here." She scribbles it down and hands it over. "I already memorized mine."

Accepting the paper, I ignore the pinch in my chest at the certainty I will never be calling her. "Thanks. It's nice to start to know people here."

She lifts the box. "It's kind of heavy."

I take it from her and frown. It won't fit into my bag with my other things. It's going to be a long walk back to the apartment.

***

It's all I can do not to stop on the street corner and open the box, but the instant I step back out into the wind, I have this sensation of being watched. Two blocks later, I still feel it and it's driving me nuts. I tell myself it's understandable paranoia considering everything, but I don't remind myself again how I got past this in New York. I didn't get past anything. I put it out of sight, and out of sight was out of mind. Not this time. This time I want answers that I hope this box holds.

Finally, I reach the apartment and with aching arms from lugging all my stuff, I walk into the hallway, drop my bag, and lock the door. Holding the box to my chest, I lean against the door and stare into the apartment, listening for anything or anyone that might be present. Eerie silence greets me, and while it should comfort me, it does not. I hate silence. I hate it with a passion. I rush forward and set the box on the table, and with my heart in my throat, I search the apartment. I lie all the time. Why should I trust the silence?

Once I'm certain I'm alone, I sit down at the dining room table, and in the absence of a kitchen knife, I struggle with the tape and use my apartment key to cut it down the center. Note to self. I need a key ring for the single key I'm bound to lose, and silverware. I need to make a kitchen list. I start one in my mind. A couple of cheap pans. Cheap paper plates. Plasticware with a few real knives. I rip the box open and set my key aside.

Lifting the lid, I stare down at the MacBook Air with a folder on top. Well, this is certainly a surprise. I reach for the folder and flip it open. A typed note is included.

> Ms. Bensen. Welcome aboard. Enclosed is a
> list of the properties Evernight leases on my
> behalf. As we discussed in our phone
> interview, you will need to do a weekly visual
> inspection to ensure they are properly
> maintained and email me a report.

Phone interview? I did a phone interview? I'm confused. This is a cover story. I was told not to look for a job. I keep reading.

An external check is all I need, and all properties are within a few blocks of one another in Cherry Creek. In addition, Evernight will provide you with a report on all newly listed properties in the Denver area. You will cross-reference them with public listings and send me anything that fits the criteria I'm including. Please email me when you get this so I know you are properly settled. I will have various other projects for you to undertake once I get to my location and get settled. I have limited phone connectivity, so if you have any issues you will need to email. If there is an emergency, you can reach my attorney, whose number I'm including.

Dermit Williams
Dermit Williams Holding Company

I scan and find an email from my new boss, and his signature, which is no signature at all. It's just his name typed. There is no script and there is no symbol to tell me I should trust this person. I'm baffled. I've been told this job is my cover story. A fake cover story. Or maybe it isn't. Maybe this is a real job, just like my lease was a real lease. The letter clearly references a conversation with someone pretending to be me. But the instructions I received clearly stated that I was not to get a job. Flipping open the folder, there really are property listings. Maybe my boss isn't real. Maybe he, like the job, is a cover that is meant to be convincing. This is not a comforting thought. It tells me I have reason to go deep into hiding.

I remove the computer from the box and find it's not new, but close. It powers right up and I create a Gmail account for Amy Bensen and email my new boss. A muffled beeping sound reminds me the phone Liam gave me is still in my bag by the door and I head that way, unpacking what items need to be removed and finding the phone lit up with a text message. Don't eat dinner. I want to take you out.

I press the phone to my forehead and try to weigh my worries for his safety as valid or not. I have no real reason to believe anyone but me is in danger, and unlike Chloe, a man like Liam has the money and resources to protect himself. But he cannot protect himself from something he doesn't know about and I do not know him well enough to risk trusting him, no matter how much my gut says I can.

The phone beeps. I look at the screen. Amy?

He's going to call me if I don't answer. I'm here. I'm doing some work my new boss gave me. Call me when you head this direction.

Your new boss?

My brows dip. Yes. My new boss.

Interesting. I can't wait to hear all about him.

Avoidance mode kicks into gear. What time will you be here?

Around six or seven. Headed into a meeting and I'm not sure how long it will take.

I glance at the clock. It's three. How did it get to be three? See you soon then.

Not soon enough.

My chest burns with what could be nothing more than a flirty message, but it feels like more. He feels like more. The very more I have ached for deep in my soul. Which is exactly why I have to walk away. I will trust him. I will pull him into my hell. And then one or both of us will crash and burn.

***

After two hours of searching the internet for clues about my new boss to no avail, I left a message for Meg about changing the locks on my apartment since the office was already closed. Trying to clear my head to think straight, I decided to shower and freshen up. For the time being, I put my shorts back on, but I will change to meet Liam. Or not. I don't know. I shouldn't change. It will send the wrong message. Seeing him again might too, but it's a risk I have to take to return the phone. I considered just dropping it off, but I feel I know enough about Liam to know he will just march to my door. If I am ending this, I need to really end it. If. No if. I am ending it. I will meet Liam at the hotel bar, nice and public, and then be on my way.

Feeling jittery, I decide to run to the store to grab a few staples, hoping it will work off my nerves. It doesn't work. Thirty minutes later, I return from the quick trip, and while I felt better while on my little excursion, I am right back where I started the instant I step into my "fake" apartment and more jittery than ever. I decide I probably need food and should force myself to eat to see if it will help, though I fear it will not sit well on my stomach. It's not like I have to worry about ruining my dinner I am not having with Liam.

Deciding on a can of soup, I pull out one of my new pans from a bag and then grimace at my newfound, should-have-been-obvious problem. I have no can opener or bowls. Paper plates are not going to cut it. Brilliant move. Just brilliant. My list has failed me and I eagerly jump on another excuse to get out of this cage I'm supposed to call home. The very idea that it will ever be that is laughable. This place is not home. Home is in Texas, where I can never return.

Considering it's already five o'clock, and Liam should be calling soon, I quickly find my way to the street. The instant I step off the elevator I know this trip is different from the last. Unease prickles through me and the hair at my nape lifts. The sensation of being watched I'd had walking to the bank earlier is back, and it is powerful. Each step I take seems to magnify the feeling. I speed up more and more, until I am all but running as I cross the main street to the grocery store.

At the door, I glance behind me, searching for the source of my discomfort, but finding no one obvious. If I could flippantly call this paranoia I would gladly do so, but I've seen death and heartache. I am not hiding from no one and for no reason. Desperately, I wish for some sign from my handler that I am safe in this new location with this new identity, but even this is troubling. I am blind to the colors around me, trapped in a world that is only black and white. Run or be caught. Hide or die. My throat thickens. Like everyone else I loved has died.

Inside the store, I begin to shop, and momentarily I am relieved. I am in a public place. I am safe and the sensation of being watched is gone, but I am deeply troubled by the idea of being watched, even by my handler. He saved my life, I remind myself. He is trustworthy. No one else can be trusted. But Liam. I play that idea over and over in my head and in every version of how and I think of all the good ways that might end. And the bad. I think of him being in danger. I think of me being in danger.

Quickly, I fill my basket, grabbing my staple bargain box of popcorn, a few bowls and a cheap can opener before I head to the checkout line. I grimace down at my basket. My popcorn requires a microwave. Craigslist or Walmart here I come and soon, I decide. Popcorn and TV dinners are this single girl's staples. I'm about to remove the popcorn from my basket to save my pennies for later, when my phone, or rather Liam's phone, rings.

Steeling myself for the impact of his voice, I answer. "Liam?"

"Damn, woman, I like how you say my name."

My cheeks heat with the gruffness of his tone that tells me that he means his words. The knowledge that I affect him reaches inside me and tightens my belly. I barely feel like I exist in this world and this rich, famous and impossibly delicious man makes me feel as if I do. I don't want to let him go. I don't want to lie to him.

"I'll be there in a couple of minutes to pick you up."

The announcement jerks me back into the moment. "I'm at the store. I'll drop off my stuff and meet you at the hotel bar."

"I'll pick you up."

"No. No. I want to change clothes anyway." It's my turn in line, and I put my items on the belt. "I have to check out. I'll see you soon."

"Amy—"

I hang up and cringe. Did I really just hang up on him? I expect him to call back but he doesn't. Maybe I should call him back but the less I say before "goodbye" the better. I can't call him back. I'm still telling myself that five minutes later when I walk out of the store with a bag that includes popcorn I cannot even pop. Another brilliant move considering my limited funds. I'm just full of them. I am less worried about who might be following me than I am who might be waiting at my door when I arrive. Crossing the parking lot, my gaze skitters here and there, watching for the stranger. Watching for him.

I am about to cross the grass to the stoplight when a fancy black sedan pulls up beside me and stops. My heart lurches and I whirl around as the passenger window rolls down, but I cannot see the driver. Holding my breath, I lean down to discover Liam occupies the driver's seat, and the man is power and sex in a black suit and a royal blue shirt that brightens his already too blue eyes. He reaches across the car and opens the door. "Hop in, baby."

My stomach flutters at the endearment that he might use on all women, but it doesn't seem to matter. Right now, he's using it on me. Right now, his eyes are on me and even in the playfulness I sense in him, they are as intense as the man. And Liam Stone is as intense as they come.

"Is this your car?" I ask, trying to decide what to do. Certain that getting in the car with him is my ticket to being mindlessly lost in the temptation that is Liam.

"Rental." He arches a brow at my stillness. "If you're worried I'll bite, I promise to tell you first."

My eyes go wide before I can stop them and he laughs, a sexy, rough sound deep from his chest. The same chest I have touched and want to touch again. I glower at him. "I won't." The smart reply earns me another of his sexy laughs, and he's successfully seduced me right here in the spot I stand.

Caving to the inevitable, I step forward and settle my bags on the floorboard of the obviously expensive car. Discreetly inhaling, I steel myself for the impact of being in a small space with him where I both long to be, but see it for what it is. A mistake. Being near this man is not going to help me say goodbye.

The instant I slide inside the car, expensive leather hugs my bare legs, and Liam's earthy scent tickles my nostrils, teasing me senseless. It's official. This was a mistake. A wonderful mistake. I tug the door shut, rotating toward Liam and I am pulled into his arms, one strong hand sliding into my hair. "Miss me?" he asks, and his breath is a hot tease on my lips.

My fingers curl on his jaw, the soft rasp of newly forming whiskers teasing my fingers. I remember that rasp on my skin. Everything fades but the moment and the man. No one has ever done that to me. "Did you miss me?"

"I'll let you decide." His mouth slants over mine, his tongue parting my lips, caressing against mine in one lush stroke. "Do I taste like I missed you?"

I am melting like chocolate in the hot sun, and he has barely touched me. But I want him to. Oh yes. I want him to. "I'm still not convinced."

His lips curve a moment before he answers me by licking wickedly into my mouth, teasing me with two deep strokes of his tongue that leave me darn near panting. "Any doubt I missed you now?" he challenges.

My chest burns with his reply. Liam missed me. I have been missed. This is unfamiliar territory and I like it. And I am so not ready to let go of this man. "If I say yes you won't kiss me again, right?"

"I'll do a whole lot more than kiss you when I get you alone." His promise is somehow both soft velvet and rough sandpaper, and the air around us shifts, thickens, the sexual tension transforming into something I cannot name, far deeper than simple lust. Far harder to walk away from. He strokes a tender hand down my hair and I lean into the touch like a cat claiming her territory when he is not mine. He will never be mine.

"Hungry?" he asks.

"Is that a trick question?"

His lips curve. "I'll take that as a 'yes'." He brushes his lips over mine. "Me too, baby. Me too." He releases me and leans back in his seat and I am instantly cold where I was hot seconds before. He puts the car in drive and cuts me a steamy blue-eyed look. "Buckle up and we'll be at your place in no time."

I don't argue, eager for anything that makes me feel grounded, certain this man will take me on a wild ride before this night is over if I let him. And I can't let him. I squeeze my eyes shut, telling myself I will not do anything but get out of this car. I will make small talk and ease the sexual tension and get back where I need to be to do what I have to do.

"There's a great Italian place next to the hotel, if you like Italian?"

My lashes lift at his question and settles on the logo on the dashboard. "I'm a pasta addict." I'm about to add "mostly Ramen noodles," but my gaze narrows on the logo on the dash and I decide he probably doesn't even know what Ramen is. "You rented a Bentley?"

He shrugs. "They didn't have anything else."

"They had nothing but a Bentley?" I don't hide my disbelief. I've never even seen a Bentley and I figure that's because they run in the six-figure range and I don't know people that pay that kind of money for a car. Really, I don't know many people who can even afford to park a car in New York, let alone pay for the vehicle.

"It's the only car I thought was good enough to drive you around in."

"Me?" I balk, pursing my lips. "You, Liam Stone, are rich and spoiled. I am not."

"I'll spoil you if you let me." His voice is a soft, silky promise.

My chest burns with something I do not want to feel. "No." It comes out almost a hiss I cannot retract. "I don't want your money." I just want a life.

If he notices my tone, he doesn't show it. "Spoken like someone who has never had money."

Avoidance is always my friend. His questions are not. "Very few people have your kind of money."

"Which shows my point." he assures me.

"Which is what?"

"I have the money to spoil you and I plan to." He doesn't give me time to argue, shifting the subject like he's stamped the topic done, approved, fact. "Do you have anything that will spoil or can we go straight to the restaurant?"

I don't want food. I want to lick that tattoo of his before I say goodbye to him. That would keep him from asking questions. Until it's over, I remind myself. "I need to drop by my place and change."

His hot gaze flickers down my bare legs, and up again. "I like you like this."

My cheeks heat and my sex clenches. "You're in a suit."

"I'll change. You stay the way you are."

I open my mouth and snap it shut before I tell him I like him just as he is. That isn't going to help my goodbye campaign, but then neither did kissing him. I try again. "Either way, I want to freshen up."

Liam pulls the car in front of his hotel and a doorman is instantly helping me out of the car. By the time I'm standing, Liam is in front of me, reaching for my bags, and he has them before I can stop him. "I've got them," I say, reaching out to take them, and darn it, our hands collide, sending a tingling sensation up my arm.

My eyes dart to his, and I see the awareness in his stare. He too has felt the connection. Maybe this is only sex to him, or some need to protect me I can't understand, but it's real. It exists and it is powerful.

"I'll meet you at the hotel bar in thirty minutes," I choke out from my suddenly dry throat.

"You said you didn't want to go to the hotel with me."

"To your room. Hotel bars are open to the public."

His eyes narrow, suspicion etched in their depths. "I'll help you with your bags."

"They're paper light. Let me hurry. I'll meet you in twenty minutes."

"I'll walk you to your door."

"If you come to my apartment, we'll get distracted." For once, I get to speak the truth.

He arches a brow. "Is that supposed to discourage me?"

"Yes," I replied tartly, and the urge to kiss him one more time before I deliver the goodbye is too intense to fight. I push to my toes and lean in to him, hands flattening on the hard wall of his chest, and press my lips to his. He is stiff, unyielding, and I am instantly uncomfortable, second-guessing my boldness. I begin to pull back when he drops my bags to the ground and pulls me close, his hand sliding up my back, his tongue licking into my mouth in one long, hot sweep that has me moaning into his mouth.

"You're no recluse," I accuse when his lips leave mine, shocked at the scene we've certainly made, embarrassed to even look around and find out who is watching.

"Or I just want to make sure you know how much I want you, no matter what the price. And you're right. If I come with you to your apartment, we won't leave anytime soon." He sets me away from him, and to my horror grabs my bags from the ground and looks inside. His gaze lifts, brow arching. "Plasticware?"

The warmth his declaration about wanting me had created turns cold. "I haven't had time to unpack."

"So your things were delivered today?"

"My things are just fine."

I reach for the bags and he shackles my wrist. "Amy—"

A horn honks, saving me whatever command is certain to come out of his too-tempting mouth. "We're making a scene. I'll see you in a few minutes."

His jaw flexes, tension etched in his face. "I'll be waiting." He releases my bags and my arm and I waste no time darting away. I am so tired of running away.

Chapter Ten

Twenty minutes later I've changed into a simple, versatile little black lace dress I scored for $29 on a bargain rack. With my heels on it's a bit sexy, but I tell myself I'm dressing up to feel confident, not to impress Liam. I'm so good at lying, I almost convince myself it's the truth. I check myself in the mirror and argue with myself about ending things with Liam. I begin with all the reasons I don't have to say goodbye. I've dated other men. I had a dorm mate, albeit we didn't bond, but we lived together. Liam can handle himself far better than anyone I have ever known. But he is also the only person I've ever known with the resources to dig into my past and get himself killed in the process. People have died. I am not hiding for no reason. He could die. I won't let that happen.

Resolve in place, I head for the elevator and ride to the bottom level. The doors ding open and I am startled to find a denim-clad Jared standing there. He grins at the sight of me, all sexy male charm and hotness. "Ditched the t-shirt, did you?"

"I did," I agree, finding myself smiling despite my nerves over Liam. I step out of the car and expect Jared to move aside to catch the door. He doesn't and we are toe to toe. The sense of familiarity with this man is instant, and I freeze, unable to move away. I am terrified, and not of Jared. Terrified of this piercing black hole that I know too well will suck me into a place where everything and everyone is a potential threat. I swore I would never return to this place but I feel the fingers of the beast reaching for me, pulling me inside.

"You're supposed to take that out of the box."

I blink Jared back into focus and the very fact that I have to says a lot about my state of mind. "Box?"

He glances down and I briefly follow his gaze to the iPhone box I wasn't able to fit into my small purse. "Oh." I lift it slightly. "This. I like the box. I'm a rebel like that."

He laughs. "A woman out to seduce me."

I snort a ridiculous sound that makes my answer all the more meaningful. "I'm the last person to seduce anyone."

His light brown eyes fill with the amusement I intended to spark. "You had me at the t-shirt and high heels," he teases.

"You are never going to let me forget that, are you?"

"Probably not." He flicks a quick look up and down my body. "Does the dress mean your things arrived okay?"

This is almost the same question Liam asked me earlier and my mood swings from comfortable in our neighborly banter to completely uneasy. I make a weak attempt at a smile. "All is well in Amy-land." I've barely spoken the lie when the cell phone begins a mocking ring from inside the box. Jared arches a brow and I quickly say, "Late to a dinner thing. I should run."

"So you have friends here already?"

I avoid a lie I might have to remember later and shrug. "I guess the t-shirt and heels were an ice-breaker. I'm going to head out. Goodnight, Jared."

"Goodnight, Amy."

There is a softer quality to his voice I now think I've heard before. I have no idea why, but something about his tone strikes a memory and a chill slides up and down my spine. Spots begin to form in front of my eyes, and oh no. No. No. No. Let it stop now. Please let this not be happening. But it's too late. The pinching sensation in my forehead I know all too well, but haven't felt in years, begins to form. I sway and Jared grabs my arm. Reflexively, my hand goes to his chest.

"Whoa," he murmurs. "What just happened?"

I can't open my eyes. I don't even try. "Blood sugar," I whisper, reverting to the excuse I'd used years before when these spells hit me. "I'm fine."

"You don't seem fine." He sounds worried. Worried is not good. Worried will get me an ambulance and attention I don't need.

I inhale and the air feels like lead in my lungs, but the pain is good. It wakes me up and brings me back. "I am." I force my lashes open and the spots begin to fade. Relief washes over me. I am already past this episode. "Really," I assure Jared. " I already feel better." Except that my hand is on his chest. Appalled, I jerk my hand back.

He chuckles. "Easy. You'll tumble over."

"No. I'm fine. I'm steady now."

He hesitates but lets my arm go. "That kind of reaction will kill a man's confidence, you know."

I doubt seriously this man has confidence issues. "Sorry. I was just embarrassed."

"Don't be embarrassed." His voice is a gentle caress.

More of that familiarity creeps into my mind and the spot in my forehead starts to tingle at the moment my phone starts to ring again. This time the sound is music to my ears, offering me a welcome escape from another episode and from Jared.

Jared's lips quirk. "You really need to ditch the box."

"Or get a bigger purse," I say, sounding like a complete idiot, which fits perfectly with me touching a stranger's chest. I am officially ready to get the heck out of here. "Thanks for the save. I'll see you around." I don't wait for an answer. For the second time today, I take off running, only this time I'm running to Liam, not away from him, and that feels so much more right than the goodbye I have to deliver with the phone in my hand.

In a short dash across the street, I approach the hotel in a gust of wind that has my dress lifting. With a gasp, I struggle to capture the skirt and juggle the phone. Somehow, I shove the material down and through the wild mass that, thanks to my new purchase, was my sleekly flat-ironed hair, I watch the doorman

THE SECRET LIFE OF AMY BENSON

smirk and nod. Cheeks heating, I hurry past him, wondering if he also witnessed Liam and me tongue dancing in front of the hotel earlier. This night is off to a grand start. I was right when I decided to change clothes. I need all the confidence I can get to survive the next fifteen minutes.

Stopping inside the doorway, I spot the sign to the restaurant/bar directly ahead. Even here, a good twenty feet away, I can already hear the rumble of voices over the sound of music coming from inside the archway entry. I might not know Liam well, but my instincts say he will not like my choice of meeting location.

As if he's heard me, Liam exits the bar, irritation etched on his handsome face, and his eyes collide with mine.

His expression softens and warms, and I watch the frustrations of moments before melt away, as if seeing me makes everything all right. I do not move to meet him, frozen in the bittersweet knowledge that seeing me has pleased him. He walks toward me, his jacket gone, his lean masculinity accented by the dark dress pants and a fitted blue shirt; he is power and grace, the epitome of dark good looks.

The instant he is before me, I am captivated by his deep, blue stare, lost in a sea of warm, drugging waters, and I do not speak. I want to swim just a little longer, but too quickly, his gaze lowers to the box I am holding and my gut twists with the knowledge that my time is up. I hold it out to him. "I can't take this." And while I am proud of how strong my voice sounds, my hand shakes, practically drawing a storyboard of my emotions that Liam is too smart to miss. Anger fills me at how the past has made me weak. I should never have taken the job at the museum and let it back into my life. But then, I would never have met Liam and I'm not sure I can wish him away, even if I have to walk away.

"Let's talk about it over dinner."

I shake my head, more at my desire to agree than at his words. "I can't go to dinner. I can't see you anymore." I sound like I mean it. Almost.

Those piercing blue eyes sharpen, and the dark edginess he wears like a second skin ramps up about a hundred notches. Seconds tick by and I try to think of some appropriate thing to say when I of all people know less is better. Should I turn and leave? Yes. I should leave. Actually, I'm still holding the phone. He needs to take the phone. He takes the phone but he doesn't stop there. He laces the fingers of his free hand with mine. "Come with me."

My eyes go wide and I don't have time to argue. He's already tugging me along with him and not toward his hotel room, and I don't have time to consider why that disappoints me. Not when he's headed toward the exit, which most likely means he intends to go to my apartment, where he will discover the delivery of my things has not taken place.

Desperation kicks in and I rush forward, putting myself in front of him, flattening the hand he isn't holding on his chest and digging in my heels. "Take me to your room." I can't even believe I've just said that, but the warm spot in my belly won't let me take it back.

Liam's jaw flexes. "You can't see me anymore but you want me to take you to my room?"

His voice is tight, a band of steel wrapping each word. He's angry. I don't know why, though the possibilities are many. I'll figure it out when we are effectively detoured from my apartment and what will surely lead him to dig where it is dangerous to dig. "Yes. Yes. I want to go to your room. I need to, ah...lick your tattoo goodbye."

"I'll keep that in mind."

My cheeks heat at the edge I've heard in his voice but I will myself past my discomfort and recover. "Liam—"

He takes a small step and I dig in my heels and wrap my fingers around his shirt, wrinkling the fine material. Direct is all I have left. "I don't want to go to my apartment."

"We aren't." This time he firmly sets me aside, and before I can so much as yelp, he has my hand in his, and we are in pursuit of the exit.

I follow eagerly, trying not to look around me, and spot attentive observers of our exchange. For a supposed recluse and a woman on the run, I'm pretty sure we've made our second scene of the day together and I'm not looking for a third. We pass the sliding glass doors and I avoid the gaze of the doorman.

Liam cuts us away from my apartment to the sidewalk on our right, where people stroll here and there, and thankfully the wind is milder and my skirt stays at my knees. I cast Liam a sideways look. "Where are we going?"

He stops abruptly and faces me. "The phone's in your name. You have to talk to them about the service."

"Oh." Disappointment hits me hard and fast. I've become complicated. He's ready to cut all ties. His "not going anywhere" vow sure didn't last. But…he's holding my hand. Why would he hold my hand if he was cutting all ties? It's not like he'd worry I'd bolt and he loses the phone. He's a freaking billionaire.

"Oh?" he prods.

"Oh," I repeat to keep myself from saying something like "can we go back to the hotel and start this night over?" when I need to stick to my plan. Saying goodbye is the right thing to do. "I'm not phone savvy," I finally manage. "If you need me to go with you I will." My gaze manages to flicker to our connected hands and the quick pinch in my chest that has me jerking my eyes back to Liam's. "Where is it?"

"Two blocks." This time, his gaze drops and not to our hands, but to my feet, where it lingers and then rakes hotly up my body. Jared's inspection this morning had been a bit too familiar. Liam's is downright wicked. And oh my, I am hot all over and tingling in places I shouldn't be tingling in public. He knows, too. I see it in the quirk of his lips, the gleam in his eyes as he asks, "Can you walk that far in those shoes?"

"After walking around New York for years, my feet are oblivious to pain. I can walk." Or I might stand here in the beam of his scorching gaze and melt in my shoes. He still wants me, but it will be cold comfort in my empty bed tonight. I'm letting him go. He's letting me go. I'm complicated. I'm always complicated.

I start to turn, to get this over with, but his fingers curl on my elbow and he pulls me close, his legs pressing to mine, sending waves of heat through me. And just like that, everything but Liam fades away. There are no people walking about, no doorman a few steps away, no horns honking. There is just me and this man, and I tingle with awareness, alive when I was barely living before meeting him. There are many things I want to say to him but cannot. I am confused and conflicted in all ways possible with this man, stuck between right and wrong.

"Liam—"

"Amy," he says softly, his tone just sharp enough to be warning, a command of silence, and maybe he simply wants me to stop arguing with him, but in my mind, he is saving me from something I might say and we both will regret.

"Yes," I say as if he's actually issued the warning, and wishing he'd say whatever he stopped me to say. Wishing it would be something magical that made everything all right. "Let's go to the store, Liam."

I do not know why I said his name. Why I felt the absolute need to say it, or why it lingered on my lips almost wistfully, but his eyes narrow, his head tilting slightly and there is no question he's noticed. I hold my breath, not sure what he will say. Not sure what I want him to say. Not sure what he intended when he pulled me close. But when he finally replies, I get nothing more than, "Yes. Let's go to the store."

Air trickles from my lips and I am both relieved and disappointed by his non-response. But he does not allow distance between us, drawing my hand in his again as he turns us forward. Easily, comfortably, we fall into step together, silence settling between us and I find myself obsessing about our fingers twined together. About what that means about his intentions and even mine.

Too quickly we are at the store and Liam releases my hand to open the door. I freeze with a jolt of reality. We are not one but two again, and he may never touch me again. Once we are done here, we are...done. Emotion wells in my chest and I can feel

Liam looking at me, willing me to look at him, but I can't. Not without forgetting why I have to do this.

Feet heavy as lead, I walk into the store, the cool air conditioning adding to the chill I have suddenly developed. Hugging myself, I stop just inside the entrance and see phone displays in the center of the store, accessories hanging on the walls and a small service counter in the back. Liam steps beside me, and as if washing away my fear he will never touch me again, his hand settles on my back. The touch is electric, sizzling down my spine and washing away the cold.

"Hi, folks." The greeting comes from a lanky guy no more than twenty, with dark, wavy hair and black, thick-rimmed glasses, wearing a store t-shirt, who stops in front of us. "I'm Scott. Can I help you?"

"We need to have you look up our account information," Liam states.

Scott shoves his glasses up his nose and indicates a counter in the back of the store. We follow him there and Liam does not remove his hand from my back. We stop at the counter and Scott walks behind it, pulling a keyboard closer to him. "What can I help you with?"

Liam sets the phone on the counter. "Can you confirm the name on the account and who has access?"

Scott's face pinches. "Only if I'm talking to the person who owns the account, and surely they would know this information already."

"Not if a good friend set the account up for them," Liam corrects.

"Then I need the ID of whoever is on the account," Scott replies. He obviously takes his job seriously and I have to respect the guy, considering how I value my privacy.

Liam glances at me. "He'll need your ID."

I'd seen this coming, but as I open my purse a sliver of unease ripples down my spine as a thought hits me. Is this Liam's way of seeing my driver's license? I remove my driver's license that reads Amy Bensen and it hits me that it is a Colorado license. Liam is a smart man. This is going to make him ask questions.

I slide the card forward face down and hold my breath in hopes that Scott is discreet. He lifts it and sets it on a keyboard beneath the counter, out of sight, and I let out a breath. He keys in my information. "What phone number do you have a question about, Ms. Bensen?"

The way he says it, like I have another one on file, is curious. I barely stop myself from asking. "I don't have it memorized."

"303-222-1018," Liam supplies by memory.

"You remembered it that quickly?"

"I'm a numbers guy."

The mental image of all those numbers trailing from his belly button down to some delicious destination I've yet to explore and never will thickens my throat. "Yes. I suppose you are."

"Got it," Scott informs us. "What do you need to know, Ms. Bensen?"

"She needs to know if anyone else is on the account," Liam answers.

Scott looks at me for confirmation and I'm not sure where Liam is going with this but I'd like to get there with him sooner than later. "Is there?"

"Nope," Scott answers. "Just you."

"And the bills go to her directly?" Liam asks.

Scott glances at me. "You can speak freely. Please tell him whatever he wants to know."

"The account is paid for a year in advance. Statements do go to you directly, Ms. Bensen, and any extra charges would therefore be payable by you."

"Does the account have a password of any type?" Liam asks.

Scott punches a key on his computer. "No password set up."

Liam opens the box and takes the phone out. "Throw that away."

"What about the paperwork?" Scott asks.

"That's why we have the internet." Liam's attention shifts to me but he speaks to Scott. "Walk her through setting it up."

Scott starts speaking, but I tune him out, focused solely on Liam. His eyes hold mine and I feel the connection between us. He never intended to return the phone. This was never about things getting too complicated. He held onto my hand to hold onto me. I should have seen that, but let my state of mind and inexperience with a man like Liam makes me a little crazy.

He steps closer to me, sweeping a strand of hair behind my ear, his fingers brushing my skin and sending a shiver down my spine. "You need the phone," he says softly. "Set up the password. You can change it at any time." He glances at Scott. "And she can change her number if she needs to as well, correct?"

"Yes," Scott agrees. "If there is a reason she needs to change it she just needs to call in and provide account validation."

Liam leans down, his hand settling possessively on my waist, branding me. I want to be branded by this man. "If you ever really want to get rid of me," he whispers, "you can always change your number."

If I ever really want to get rid of him. He didn't believe my lie. I didn't either.

***

A few minutes later, I've tucked my cell phone into my pocket and let Liam hold the door for me to exit the store. Pausing, I wait for him to join me, instinctively scanning the still-busy sidewalk illuminated by a combination of moonlight and street lanterns.

"How about that dinner?" Liam asks, stepping beside me, and just that easily I've forgotten my surroundings and there is only him.

"Earlier," I start, "back at the hotel. Liam, when I said what I said. I…" Still need to say goodbye, but I can't seem to get the words out.

He steps closer to me, sliding his hand to my face. "If you tell me you don't want to be with me. I will listen. I won't like it, but I'll listen. I need you to know that. But when you say you

103

'can't' be with me, like some obstacle out of your control is stopping you from seeing me, I'm not going to listen."

I am stunned and happy and confused and freaked out all at once. It is as if he has reached inside my head and ticked off every possible thing I could need him to say but it also means he sees too much. And yet…not enough. I have never wanted to bare my soul to anyone and I do now to a man I barely know.

"Liam—"

He brushes his lips over mine, and while I have no idea what was going to come out of my mouth, I think this is another case of him saving me from saying something we both might regret. "Let's go eat, baby."

Let's go eat, baby. I like how familiar this sounds. How not alone it makes me feel. "Yes," I whisper, willing accepting the reprieve I am certain he has intentionally offered me. "Let's go eat."

His eyes light with approval, his fingers lacing with mine, and in silent agreement we begin to walk and my mind replays that first time I'd seen Liam in the airport. Even from across a room, he'd spoken to me. I think of making love to him. I think of him picking me up today from the store and then kissing me in front of the hotel. I think of every second I've spent with this man, so absorbed that I blink and we are stopped at a restaurant a few doors down from Liam's hotel. Suddenly, I realize that for all of my thinking I managed on this walk, remarkably, there's one thing I haven't had on my mind. Godzilla. I have not thought about what monster is watching or lurking around the corner. And Liam did that for me.

He holds the door to the restaurant open for me and for a moment I just stare at him, this brilliantly talented, amazingly generous man, who epitomizes tall, dark, and handsome, and I think I am crazy. Crazy for him. And I'm selfish. So very selfish because I have been alone and now he is here and I don't know how I can walk away from him. I don't deserve him and he absolutely does not deserve me.

Chapter Eleven

Ten minutes after arriving for our reservations at North, a chic modern restaurant with frosty dangling lights and steel and glass tables, Liam and I are sitting inside a high-backed half-moon-shaped booth that seems to hug us in privacy. Our twenty-something attractive blonde waitress takes our orders of pasta and salads, batting her eyes at Liam in the process, clearly smitten with him, but then so are most of the females in the place from what I could tell on our arrival. He, however, is a perfect, suave gentlemen, neither disrespectful to her nor encouraging for that matter, casting me warm looks in the process. I am charmed and remarkably at ease with her flirtation considering my inexperience and his good looks.

Reluctantly the woman tears her eyes from Liam and departs, and a waiter appears by our table with the insanely expensive bottle of champagne Liam has ordered for us. Once the top has been popped and our glasses are filled, Liam and I are finally alone.

Liam lifts his glass, shifting in his seat to stare down at me and his blue eyes might as well be red fire, they burn so hot. "To new friends and lovers."

Goose bumps lift on my skin at the intimacy of his words, ripples of awareness tingling across my chest, down to my belly, and I am blown away by how easily Liam affects me. No one has ever come close to doing this to me, but then, I know the sweetness of his mouth on mine. The perfection of his body intimately molded against me. I know what it is like to fall asleep in his arms.

I clink my glass to his, but I cannot repeat the sultry words of his toast. Liam waylays my escape, reaching forward as my hand withdraws, and gently shackles my wrist. He arches a dark brow and his face is etched in silent reproach and yes, challenge. This man challenges me at every turn. Irrationally, nerves flutter in my stomach. I have been naked with Liam, with my fingers laced behind my back, and somehow, I feel more naked here and now than I did then. But I am so very tired of hiding from everything, most especially myself. And somehow hiding from me is hiding from him.

Delicately, I clear my throat. "To new friends and lovers," I repeat, and I watch the approval in his eyes, and suddenly I know what feels different about this moment than when we'd been making love, or rather, fucking, as Liam has called it. Here, in public, there is no veil of spontaneity to hide behind, and in this moment, there is no lie spoken to deny what is burning between us. This is the most intimate I have been with this man, or any man for that matter.

We both sip our champagne and the bubbles blossom in my mouth, both tart and sweet, like this night with Liam. Like everything with Liam. "Good?" he inquires.

I nod and set my glass down and he does the same. "It's delicious."

"So are you."

Blood rushes to my cheeks and I am so out of my safe zone it's not even funny. Or maybe it is, considering I cannot stop the nervous laughter bubbling from my lips. "If someone had told me I would be sitting in Denver, having dinner with a gorgeous prodigy billionaire architect tonight who'd be giving me compliments, I'd have suggested they needed medical attention." I reach for my champagne and sip.

"I'm not a recluse. I just wish I could be sometimes."

"And the most bizarre part of that reply is your arguing that you aren't a recluse. Billionaire"—I lift my hand—"no argument there."

He sets his glass down, and his hand goes to my leg, sending darts of heat up my thigh. "I am what I am."

It is a sobering statement and, probably compliments of the champagne, I cannot seem to hold back a wistful reply of, "That's an enviable trait."

"And that means what?"

I down my champagne and he arches a surprised brow. I'm pretty surprised myself. I value a tightly controlled tongue. "I don't drink much and I haven't eaten all day so that probably wasn't smart."

"If it makes you stop being afraid to speak your mind to me, then it was a good choice."

I don't play dumb. I probably have the champagne to thank for that, too. "You're intimidating."

"No. Not to you."

"So you agree you're intimidating."

"To some people but not to you. I'm not your Godzilla, baby, and we both know it."

"No. No, you aren't. Far from it." I pause and wait, testing him. Will he push me for the answers he swears he can wait for? He doesn't ask. Instead, he arches his brow again, the look in his eyes clearly saying "did I pass the test?"

"You really aren't going to ask, are you?"

"I told you—"

"Tell you when I'm ready."

"Exactly." He fills my glass and hands it to me.

"Are you trying to get me drunk?"

"Yes. Then maybe you'll feel ready."

I laugh. "You're very…honest."

His thumb strokes my cheek, tender and sensual. "Raw and honest, baby. Remember?"

This is a repeating theme with him, and while I've let guilt make the words about me, I wonder if they are really more about him. "Who made you hate lies?"

"Doesn't everyone?"

"That's a deflection." I know because I'm so damn good at it.

Surprises flickers in his eyes and he sets his glass down. "Money breeds lies, baby. They swim like sharks all around me."

More deflection, but it tells me more about him than perhaps he realizes. About us. Outwardly we are night and day, but I now know why we share what has felt like an instant bond. We sense what is beneath the surface of each other, and it is the same. Everyone in his world he once loved is gone. Everyone who still lives wants something from him.

I reach up and touch his cheek. "I don't want your money."

His hand covers mine. "I know."

"The phone—"

"Was a gift to me. It gives me piece of mind that you're safe." His lips curve. "And maybe you'll even feel a little obligated to answer my calls, though I'm not gambling on that."

I barely register the joke, but rather the concern beneath it. No one shows concern for me and I do not take it for granted. Regretting the buzz in my head, I set my glass down, done with the bubbles. "I'm serious, Liam. You spent a lot of money on me. I need you to know that I'm not one of those people—"

He leans in and kisses me. "I do know."

"You didn't let me finish."

"You don't have to. I know you aren't one of those people. I don't let those people in." His voice lowers, roughens. "You're in, Amy."

I am stunned by his absolute statement. "You barely know me."

His lips curve. "I can think of all kinds of ways we can remedy that, with and without clothing."

My lips curve. "You are a very bad billionaire."

"I think you like that."

"I don't think I know enough to be sure."

"Then we'd better find out."

I shock myself by saying, "Tonight?"

His eyes gleam with approval. "Oh yeah, baby. Tonight."

Tonight. The word lingers in the air and there is a silent understanding between us in a way I have never shared with anyone. We both know that I've just erased the question of where this night will end, and it will not be with me alone, regretting a goodbye we both know I never wanted to say. I'll convincingly feed him what my file says I should and then he won't look into my background. Lies to protect him that handle the here and now. I'll figure out the later, when I have some time alone.

A woman delicately clears her throat and Liam and I reluctantly break apart, our eyes lingering on each other's a moment before our salads are placed in front of us. Beneath the table, Liam's hand settles back on my leg, his thumb stroking my knee, and I feel every caress in my sex. I do not want food. I want Liam.

"Need anything else right now?" the waitress asks.

Liam glances my direction, giving me a look at that says, "You're my dinner", as he replies, "Not right now."

The instant she's gone I scold him. "Liam."

He leans in and kisses me. "Liam, what?"

My mouth goes dry. "You have to behave."

"Always or just right now?"

"Just right now."

A low laugh rumbles from his chest and he hands me my silverware. "I'll behave so you can eat. I've been here a few times in the past and never been disappointed."

"When you designed the building you mentioned downtown?" I ask, and I am not afraid of my questions sparking his questions anymore. I believe Liam. He will let me answer what I want to answer. I'll figure out what that means later. Not tonight. Tonight has been decided. I am with him and the rest of the world does not exist.

"Yes. I was here a couple of months and stayed in this area."

A couple of months. My vow to focus on just tonight evaporates and I make a pretense of picking up my fork and picking at my salad to hide how crazy my mind is going. Will he be here that long this time? And what if I get attached to him and he goes back to New York? He will go back to New York and I can't even visit him there. That will be when the file isn't enough anymore. Raw and honest, he keeps saying. Why can't I not just have that with one person in my life?

"Hey," he says softly.

I swallow the knot in my throat and glance up at him. "Hey."

"What just happened?"

I don't have an answer so I don't offer one. "I was just wondering about your meeting. How did today go?"

He narrows his eyes and studies me a moment and I do not know what he sees, but it's probably too much. "Better than it should have," he finally says. "And they have you to thank for that."

"What does that mean?"

"I've decided to stay around a while. If I can create something I'm excited about in the process I'd like to."

"You're staying?"

"Yes. I'm staying. Any problem with that?"

I've proven I don't have coy or goodbye in me with this man. Why change either now? "I won't complain about seeing more of you."

His eyes light with approval. "That's good to hear, considering you were ready to kick me to the curb earlier."

"I wasn't. I just…" I need more time to think about what to say to him. "Did they like your design?"

He plays dodgeball like the pro I am. "All but one of the investors, who is a complete prick."

"You like him that much, huh?"

"Yes. That much."

"What don't you agree on?"

"Everything."

"Everything?"

"He still wants the tallest building in existence."

I remember his comment on the plane and smile. "Is he short?"

He laughs and it is so warm and wonderful that I could roll around in it like sunshine on a cold day. "Actually, yes," he says. "He is."

"Hmmm," I say, pondering. "That doesn't sound good. So what do you think? Will you find a compromise with him?"

"Too many people involved want my name, and skill, attached to the project to not try to make this work." Amazingly, I think, as he continues, he doesn't sound arrogant, but matter-of-fact. "Two of the biggest financial investors won't arrive until Monday. If I win them over with my design, then it's probably a done deal. I'll still need to meet with the engineers and make sure everyone is on the same page, but all in all, I'm probably only a week from a decision."

I know that he's said he's staying, but some part of me aches for further confirmation. "So I get you for at least a week?"

"I told you, baby. Deal or no deal. I'm not in any rush to leave."

I am too relieved, too emotionally dependent on someone I barely know, and I do not understand why. I have had no one. I have relied on me. What is it about this man that makes me want to lean on him, and is that good or bad?

"Food is here," the waitress announces, and feeling exposed and vulnerable for reasons I can't quite understand, I take the excuse to look away from Liam, as she adds, "And I'm sorry I didn't give you much time on the salads. The kitchen was fast."

It's not long before we are sipping more champagne and enjoying our pasta dishes, but I have a raw nerve still bleeding vulnerability I cannot seem to seal. Reflexively, I launch into my standard question-asking strategy meant to prevent question answering. Easy to do with Liam when I crave every detail I can learn about him. "Will you tell me about how you started apprenticing at such a young age?"

"The real story or the one I tell the media?"

"There are two versions?"

He sips his champagne. "One for the press. One for me."

I stab a bite of pasta. "I'll take both, please."

"I had a feeling you would. Alex met me at a public event and learned of my interest in architecture and took me under his wing."

"And the real story?"

"What makes you think that isn't it?"

"Is it?"

His jaw hardens. "No. The real story is that I was obsessed with drawing buildings and I told my mother I wanted to be a famous architect."

"How old were you when this started?"

"Per my mother's old stories, I was six. At thirteen I hadn't stopped talking about it and had stepped up my interest. I was trying to self-teach via books. My mother heard Alex was in the city unveiling a building, and despite working two jobs at the time, she found the time and means to get me there. We were living in the Bronx. And that's when I met Alex and he saw something in me." He goes on to tell me all about going to Alex's house on weekends and summers.

Until this moment, I had not let myself connect the dots of his past to mine. I too, had been a child protégé to my gifted father, and I reach for my champagne to keep from letting the confession fall from my lips. That was my old life, my real life. Amy Bensen has a business degree. She didn't have a famous archeologist for a father. Dead father. My father is dead.

"Alex tortured me with hours upon hours of math equations," he continues, and I set down my glass, saved from my past by my interest in his.

"I hate math." Although his tattoo could make me change my mind. My lips curve. "You seem rather fond of it."

His eyes gleam with understanding. "Alex used tell me there were infinite possibilities in life and architecture. The tattoo represents that to me."

Infinite possibilities in life. I am not sure I like that idea. How many people will I be before I die?

"Of course," Liam adds, "as a kid I just wanted to draw buildings. Alex said that's what you call an artist, not an architect. I fought the math, and ended up doing the whole wax on, wax off thing like in Karate Kid."

I laugh. "Karate Kid? But that was to learn karate. What did that have to do with math?"

"It's hard work. My punishment for not getting the math right and complaining about having to try." He laughs, but it's laced with a hollow sadness. "And he liked the movie." He smiles, shifting out of the past to the present. "I don't like the movie. I do, however, like math now. Funny how mastering something makes you change your tune about it. By the time I was in college I was a whiz."

The waitress takes my plate and I am shocked to realize it is all but empty. A few minutes later, we are enjoying coffee and I sigh in contentment, more relaxed than I have been in a very long time. "What did your parents think about Alex?" I ask, not ready for this dinner to end.

"My mother adored him."

"And your father?"

His expression turns somber. "He wasn't around to have an opinion."

"I want to ask. I'm not sure I should."

He gives me a wry smile. "And that's about as honest as it gets."

He's right. It is and it feels good, but what I sense in him does not. "Do you want to tell me?"

"He ran out on us when I was eight," he says easily. Almost too easily. "Told me he was going to the store and never came back."

"You grew up poor." There is so much more to this man than billionaire architect. "That's why your mother worked two jobs."

"Yes. Until Alex came along. He took care of my mother."

113

"Did they date?"

He gives a quick shake of his head. "No. They were just close friends and when she came down with cancer, Alex paid for her treatment."

I blink. "What? Cancer?"

"Cervical. She didn't have the money for regular checkups so it was caught late, but she beat it twice."

My throat thickens at the obvious. She didn't beat it three times. "How old were you?"

"Fifteen. Alex adopted me."

"Alex lost his kids and you lost your parents."

"Yes. Exactly."

"And Alex? You said you lost him, too?"

"He had a heart attack while I was chasing pyramids a couple of years back."

He cuts his gaze and reaches for his coffee, and I sense his internal emotional battle and do not know the right thing to say or do. I just sit there until his gaze lifts and collides with mine. And I see the truth in his eyes. "You don't talk about this."

"No."

"But you did to me."

"Yes. Now ask me why."

"Why?"

"Someone has to go first."

It is what he said to me on the plane. It is his offering of trust, and I know I was right. There is something happening between us, something I may never experience again, and ironically that means lying. Now, this moment, is my chance to tell him Amy Bensen's story. To make sure he doesn't dig around to find out on his own.

I open my mouth to relay my fake life per my Amy Bensen file, and snap it shut with a stunning realization. My story is Liam's story. Her father ran out on her when she was a kid and her mother died of cancer. How can this be? It's impossible. I am not telling this lie to Liam. I can't. I won't.

"I need to go to the ladies' room," I say, and I do not wait for his reply. I scoot out of the booth and take my purse with me, but Liam is out the other side and standing in front of me, and I see the worry in his eyes. It's like he senses my instinct to bolt. He thinks I'm running away, and I am—but not from him. From the me I don't even recognize as me.

"Amy—"

I lean into him and press to my toes, brushing my lips over his. "I still want to lick your tattoo. Remember?"

But he doesn't laugh. He leans back and gives me an intense look. "Hurry back and let's get out of here."

"Yes. I'd like that."

His hands slowly ease from my waist where they have settled, reluctantly it seems, and I like that he does not want to let me go. And I do not want him to either, but I have to find a way to make this work.

I rush away from Liam, and the waitress directs me to the bathroom, a fancy three-stall room with mirrors on the door, and I rush inside the farthest one and lock myself inside. All too soon, I am back where I was two nights ago, leaning on a bathroom stall and fretting. But this time Liam has found me and I do not want to lose him or put him in danger. I tell myself lies protect him and I should embrace them and him while he is in Denver. But deep down I feel this man inside me and I do not want to limit our possibilities. He knows I'm running and if I really want to be with him, I have to ensure he does not dig into my background. If I don't give him something, he might go look on his own.

The air shifts in the bathroom and I push off the wall. I didn't hear the door open but I hadn't heard it at the museum either. My hand goes to my throat and I do not dare breathe. I listen and I do not hear anything. Wait. Do I? Time seems to stand still and I can't seem to make myself move. What if I go outside the stall and there is another note? What if I have to run?

The cell phone in my purse starts to ring and I jerk at the sound. It's Liam. Of course, it's Liam. He is the only one who has my number. How long have I been standing here? I shake myself and open the stall, steeling myself for whatever I find outside. Eager to just know what waits on me, I rush forward and stop dead in my tracks as I bring the sinks into view.

"Meg? What are you doing here?"

She whirls around from where she stands at the sink primping her long blond hair to lie on her shoulders, a contrast to her short red dress. "Oh my gosh. Amy! What are you doing here?"

"I…" My phone starts ringing again.

"Oh good." She lights up. "You got your phone working. I can't believe we're both here."

"I…yes. Very small world."

"That's what I love about this little area of Cherry Creek. You can live, eat, shop, and play here and get to know everyone like it's a small town. Only we have Chanel and Gucci in this small town. We're the high-society chicks. Well, not that I can afford that kind of thing, but maybe I'll find me a sugar daddy."

I cringe considering Liam and his billionaire status and think that while her comment is playful, he must deal with real-life money chasers. "Are you on a date?"

"My boss brought me. And he's certainly a hot property himself. What about you?"

"Yes. A date. Who I should get back to."

She grabs her purse and pulls out her phone. "Let me grab your number before we forget."

I can't get out of this. Dang it. I remove my phone from my purse and glance at the numbers on the screen and my throat goes dry. One is from Liam. The other is unknown.

Chapter Twelve

I stare at the unknown number and my mind races. It could be a wrong number. It has to be. No one has this number but Liam and my handler has never called me. That's not true, I remind myself and my mind flashes back.

The phone is ringing and I jerk to a sitting position. There is no one left to call me. No one I love. It has to be one of them. Someone is alive. This is all a mistake. I grab the headset and my hand shakes so hard I all but drop the receiver. "Dad?"

"Listen and listen quickly, Amy," a stranger says. "They are coming for you. Get up and get dressed and get the hell to the back door of the hospital. I'll be in a cab waiting for you."

"What? Who are you?"

"There isn't time. Get the hell out of the fucking bed. Now!"

"Okay, ready," Meg announces. "What's the number?"

I blink through spots, and damn it, my eyes are prickling and my forehead pinching. Meg waves her phone in front of me. "I'll type it in my phone so I can't lose it."

"Right," I croak and try to smile, though I imagine I look like I just swallowed a rock the lump in my throat is so big. Somehow, I lift my phone and punch in the screen to see my number, then read it to her.

"Perfect," she declares, and if she notices I'm rattled, she doesn't show it. "I'll call you tomorrow and we'll make a date."

"Great. Yes."

She heads towards the door and I follow her into the hallway, where she has halted, a stunned look on her face. And I know why. Liam is leaning on the wall, looking to her, I am sure, like some sort of magazine model or romance hero who has miraculously popped off the pages of a novel. His eyes meet mine and I feel the connection inside and out, radiating. To me, Liam is what he has seemed since our plane ride. Salve on an open, aching wound.

He pushes off the wall the instant he sees me and pulls me to him. "I was worried about you."

"He's with you?" Meg asks from behind me, and there is no missing the shock etched in her voice. I refuse to read into it.

Liam answers for me. "Yes. I'm with her."

Meg whistles and I turn in Liam's arms, comforted by the way his hand settles on my stomach and pulls my back to his chest. "Amy, honey," Meg declares, "I need to know where you shop. I'll call you tomorrow." She darts down the hallway and I stare after her, fighting the urge to follow her to ask her boss about my new boss, unsure I am steady enough to even try.

"She'll call you tomorrow?" Liam asks, and I turn to him.

"She's the secretary at the leasing office. She wants to do coffee or drinks." My hand settles on the hard wall of his chest and warmth travels up my arms and over my chest and shoulders.

"Then why do you look like you saw a ghost?"

I laugh but it sounds choked. "I guess ghosts are like lies. They swim like sharks all around me." What was intended as a joke holds so much truth that I am shocked I have allowed such a telling statement to fall from my lips. I am even more shocked that I cannot seem to regret it.

He studies me, his eyes probing, and I sense he wants to ask questions, but he doesn't. Damn it, he doesn't and I want him to ask, just as I want to answer. "Sharks only have the power you give them, baby. Own them. Don't ever let them own you. And they'll have to fight me to get to you anyway."

Suddenly, I am swimming in one part fantasy, one part wicked, hot desire. His declaration checks every box on my fairy tale desire list and strokes my need for him to a full on fire. And while his words might be pure seduction, I choose to grant them the possibility. I choose the fantasy. The escape he has proven he can be for me in a way no one else ever has been.

He leans in and presses his mouth to my ear. "I'm going to take you to my room now, and fuck you until neither of us can walk anymore." He eases back, searching my face for a reaction, his blue eyes blazing hot through the dim lighting of the hallway. "Any objections?"

"No," I whisper, and am shocked at how unabashedly I reply to his wicked declaration. "No objections whatsoever." Not only do I want this man, I have no doubt, for at least tonight, he can make me forget the phone call. He can make me forget everything but him.

"Then let's get out of here." He caresses a path down my arms, raising goose bumps on my arms and I am anything but cold. In fact, the only time I am not cold is in this man's presence. His fingers lace with mine, and as he leads me forward, this intimate act of hand-holding that is becoming familiar, creates a burn in my chest and a moment of fear. I could get used to this. I could get used to him in my life, by my side.

Entering the main dining room, I am momentarily jerked back into the world where he is not all there is and where the ghosts that swim like sharks at my feet, and in my head, live. I scan for Meg and her boss, but I do not see her, or him. Relief washes over me. I do not want to think of anything right now but Liam's wicked promise.

***

The walk to the hotel is silent. We don't have to speak. The air between us is both electric and soothing, a contrast that speaks to my soul. This is what I need. He is what I need. I refuse to let anything else in. I will not melt down in a haze of pain and heartache, or fear over a phone call. I can worry about that tomorrow. Locked in Liam's room I am safe, and in his arms my escape will be complete.

119

And when we approach the entrance of the hotel, I do not even make a pretense of my mockery of a story about fearing how I will look to the hotel staff. Maybe I should care for other reasons. Maybe I should fear being noticed, and with Liam, it is impossible not to be noticed, but I do not. I am with Liam and I will not be any other way in this moment of time.

"Mr. Stone," the doorman greets Liam with a nod.

Liam inclines his chin at the man and I find myself drinking in his profile, so strong, so confident, and I envy him, this man who knew what he wanted to be in life and made it happen. This man who knows where he has been and who he is. I know nothing of me, not even where I have really, truly been and why I am here. Why I exist. Why I breathe. We are not alike, as I had kidded in the restaurant. We are so different that we are top and bottom, night and day, but when I am in his arms, I do not have to face these things or myself.

The short path through the lobby to the elevator feels eternal, and I am unusually frustrated when the doors to the car open and we have to wait for someone else to exit. Liam seems to mimic my urgency, pulling me into the car before I can walk in myself, and then pressing me toward the wall by the keypad, his big body framing mine.

My hands go to his chest and heat darts up my arms and across my chest. Liam slides a card into an elevator slot, directing us to the penthouse level, and then flattens a hand on the wall above my head. Our eyes connect and I feel it clear to my toes, in every part of me. Still we do not speak, as if we are both afraid the spell will be broken and we will be back to goodbye.

The doors ding open and he drags his hand down my arm, and laces my fingers with his, tugging me along again as if he fears I will change my mind. After my flip-flopping from no to yes, I don't blame him, but that is over. I crave the hot, dominant way I know he will take me away. I want to be here, to be with him.

A quick swipe of his keycard and the door is open, and he flips the light on. Liam tugs me inside and I smile as we step toe to toe, his hands on my shoulders. "Any second thoughts?" he challenges.

"About how this night started, yes. About now, none."

"Do you want to talk about how it started?"

"Do we have to?"

"No." He takes my hand. "We don't have to talk about it."

A charge sparks in the air and he starts backing down the hallway and I willingly follow until the sound of my phone ringing freezes me in place. Urgency is like lightening in my blood, my future hanging on the unanswered line. "I have to get this." I tug my hand from Liam's and grab my purse from my shoulder, unzipping it with an obvious shake to my hand that Liam isn't going to miss.

Aware that I am unsteady, a mix of champagne and panic, I lean against the wall and stare down at the unknown number. Quickly, I punch the "answer" button before I miss the call again, and I swear my heart is about to explode through my throat as I croak, "Hello."

"Ms. Bensen?"

"Yes."

"Oh, good," a slightly familiar male voice proclaims. "This is Scott from the cell phone store. You left your driver's license here. We close in an hour if you want to swing by."

Relief washes through me and nervous laughter, once again, bubbles from my lips. "Thank you. I'll come by tomorrow and get it."

"I'll hold it at the register and keep it safe. Goodnight."

"Thank you again. Goodnight." I end the call and Liam takes my phone and shoves it back into my purse before setting it on the ground and the look in his eyes says I'm in for another game of dodgeball I do not want to play.

"I left my ID in the store." I lean forward and wrap my arms around Liam's neck and mold my upper body to his. Warmth spreads from every place we are touching to every place we are not. "Where were we?"

His hand splays between my shoulder blades, a hot branding
I welcome, but the warning that follows is ice dousing the fire.
"You aren't going to pretend what just happened didn't happen.
Just like you aren't going to tell me you didn't walk into the
bathroom at the restaurant running from me and then exit
running from someone, or something, else. And I'm not buying it
was Meg."

"New places make me nervous." I press my lips to his.

His hand tangles in my hair and gently pulls my head back,
forcing my gaze to his, and his eyes are as hard as his voice as he
orders, "Don't give me that kind of answer. Raw and honest,
Amy. That's what we are or we are nothing at all." He presses me
against the wall, caging me with his arms, pinning me in a stare.
"Tell me who is scaring you and I promise you, Amy, I will make
them go away."

If only it were that easy. If only he could be my Prince
Charming, my hero. But the truth he wants is that I'm a reality
show kind of gal. And in reality, heroes die, just like everyone else
in my life. I grab his shirt and lean into him. "What happened to
you fucking me until we can't walk anymore? That's what tonight
is supposed to be. Not you making me one of your mathematical
equations you have to crack. I don't want to be cracked, Liam. I
don't want to answer questions. I want to be fucked." I barely
recognize the woman who can say such a thing and that only
twists me into a few more knots. I am sick of not knowing. "You
promised. You said you were—"

I yelp in surprise as he picks me up and starts walking. "What
are you doing?"

"No more questions, remember?"

Blood rushes to my ears, and I do not even try to see the
room around me but I am aware it's a fancy sitting area that is
nothing more than a means to an end. The bedroom. Sex. We are
going to have sex. That's what I asked for. That's what I dared to
demand. Actually, I demanded I be fucked. Until last night, I
didn't say that word. This man is changing me and I am not sure
if that is good or bad. It feels good. He feels good, but maybe too

good. I cannot even willingly lie to the man when lying is how I survive. He is making me careless. He is making me...so much. Too much. Not enough when I want more, and I have no business wanting anything at all.

We enter the bedroom and a light glows dimly, though I am not aware of how or when Liam turned it on, and to my surprise, he bypasses the bed that sits in the center of the main wall of the room. Instead, he sets me on my feet in front of a massive bathroom I barely glimpse, before he shuts the door. And that intense edginess I'm coming to know as Liam has cranked up several notches. He is mad or...wounded? Over me? That can't be. He is confident and experienced and I am...whatever I am, but I am less, if I have hurt this man who has already proven he is so much more than his Wiki page.

"Liam—"

"No more talking." His hands come down on my waist, a possessive branding, and his voice is hard, a tight band I have the impression might break with his mood at any moment. He walks me backwards several steps until my heels hit the door and I lean against the hard surface. His legs shackle mine, holding me as captive as the burn in his eyes. "You want me to fuck you, Amy, I'll fuck you."

I think he is angry and suddenly, the word "fuck" feels like a slap when I am the one who all but shouted it at him. "Yes. Yes, I do, but—"

His mouth comes down hard on mine, hot with demand, with anger. I do not want him to be angry and I lean into him, hoping it will fade, hoping to get lost in him, but it doesn't work. I taste the bite of his mood, the roughness of his tongue, and I shove at his chest and tear my mouth from his. "Wait. Not like this."

"You want to fuck or you don't. I am not a yo-yo any more than you are one of my mathematical equations."

"Don't say it like that."

"Don't challenge me to fuck you and then run away."

Run away. I am always running away and sick of that being my life. "You're just"—I make myself look at him—"you're you, Liam, like you said I'm…me. And you, Liam Stone, are like a bull when you want something. You charge."

"What I want is you."

Even though I know this, hearing it stirs a sweet spot in my belly and all I want to do is savor the sensation and the man who created it. "Then please. Just be with me. Just be with me, Liam."

He wraps his fingers around my neck and pulls me to him. "I get wanting to block things out. Been there, done that, baby, but I won't let you do it to me. We're going to talk tomorrow, but tonight, we'll forget." He brushes his lips over mine and I feel myself tremble from the simple, but powerful touch. "Now. Turn around." He doesn't give me time to respond, rotating me to face the door, my hands on the hard surface, and I am beginning to think he likes me like this. I think I might like me like this. He leans into me, his body deliciously heavy and hard, his breath a warm seduction against my neck as he declares, "No more barriers," and tugs my zipper down, though I do not think he is talking about clothes.

I was kidding myself to challenge him to "fuck" me, to think sex is my sanctuary from words with Liam when I am headed deeper into this web of intimacy with him, a place where he will want, and even deserve, answers to all of his questions. But as his hands glide my dress down my shoulders, leaving goose bumps in their wake, I find it hard to care. He promised to take me away and I believe he can. Already, I am sinking into the sweet oblivion of pleasure that only Liam has ever helped me find. He is my sanctuary from everything else. He alone is my escape.

"Step," he commands, and I lift my feet one after another and let him kick my dress away. Then I squeeze my eyes shut when he unhooks my bra, and I shrug out of it, and just like that, I am, as I was only one night before, naked before this man, my breasts swollen and heavy, my nipples tight balls of aching need. His hands flatten on the wall by my head but he does not touch me. He likes this, I think. To trap me. To be in control. And I like it. I like him being in control instead of the world outside. I like that when I hand control to him there is pleasure, not pain.

"Turn back around," he commands, and I like that, too. The roughness of his voice, the absoluteness of him being in charge. I do not hesitate to comply. I face him, and his gaze does a hot up-and-down inspection of my naked body, that sizzles every nerve ending I own.

"Take off the shoes."

I kick them off.

"Now the panties and the thigh-highs. I want nothing between us."

But he is fully clothed. "Are you...?"

"When you ask questions, I ask questions."

I swallow hard at the pointed remark and the clear message he intends. He knows that's what I do. He knows I play dodgeball, and with anyone else it would work. With him, I've already run out of rope. I shove aside the worry this creates inside me and focus on just what I told him. Tonight. An escape. With him.

I roll down my thigh-highs and toss them away, and waste no time with my panties. I am naked before this man but I am so much more. I am exposed, vulnerable, and somehow I feel protected and safe.

"On your knees," he orders softly.

"My knees?"

"No questions, baby. You do what I say."

I inhale and hold in the air. I trust Liam. I trust Liam. When was the last time I said that about anyone? I lower myself to my knees, the soft carpeting padding my bare skin. Liam squats in front of me. "Hands over your head and on the door handle."

This time I gulp. I cannot believe I am doing this, but I do. I curl my fingers around the knob above my head, and now I am truly exposed, my breasts thrust high, my body stretched out for his viewing. But he does not look at my body. He watches my face, searching my eyes, an intense, inscrutable look etched in the hard lines of his handsome face.

He loosens his tie, then pulls it from his neck. Adrenaline surges through me with the certainty that his shirt and pants are next, but he does not undress. He reaches over me to my wrists, and I gasp at the realization that Liam is using his tie to bind my arms over my head.

I am more than naked and vulnerable. I am at his mercy.

Chapter Thirteen

Willingly tied to the door and at his mercy, I am remarkably without fear, and there is a burn in my belly. Cool air conditioning teases my nipples, a striking contrast to the heat in Liam's gaze as it rakes over my body. The tie is snug silk on my wrists, a promise I cannot escape whatever Liam intends for me. I do not want to escape what he intends for me. Anticipation is liquid fire between my thighs. I am aroused, wet, and aching with an emptiness only he can fill. It is beyond erotic to allow him this control, and for someone who often feels I do not know myself, I am suddenly aware of why his control pleases me. When I am with him like this, I don't have to calculate what comes next. He will do that. He is doing that. I trust him to the degree of allowing myself to be tied up with my hands over my head, when I do not trust anyone.

Finally, Liam begins to undress, and I am spellbound by this powerful, sexy man, downright hungry to see him completely naked, stripped down in all his masculine glory, a pleasure I didn't have the night before. There was just us ripping whatever clothes off we could to come together. This time is slower, more luxurious.

He toes off his shoes and slides his jacket down his shoulders. Almost impatiently, it seems, he unbuttons his shirt. Or maybe it is simply me who is impatient. Adrenaline pours through me as dark, springy hair peeks from the fine material and finally, his shirt is gone. My mouth goes dry at the sight of taut skin over flexing muscle and when his hand goes to his pants, I suck in a breath and I do not breathe again until he is without clothes, standing before me, his thick erection pulsing thickly in front of him.

I take in the sight of him, tall and finely carved, and he is truly a work of art, the definition of masculine beauty but I hone in on my obsession, one that I am sure many women have shared. The tattoo. My gaze tracks the path of the equation that trails down, down, down, and I swallow hard at where it ends and he is, ah, well, hard. Liam has singlehandedly made math sexy for a girl who has despised every number she's ever met.

Liam turns away and my heart thunders in my chest as he opens a dresser drawer and I anticipate what he might produce, but I am remarkably unafraid for a woman tied to a door. I am quite sure I should be, though. What if it's a whip or chains, or…what do people do when they tie up a lover? He pulls out a box and a pinch begins in my chest as I digest the packaged condom he's removed from inside. I am suddenly excruciatingly insecure, aware that there have been many before me, few before him.

He tears open the package, and I drop my head between my shoulders, hiding the emotions expanding where the pinch had been. I am not sure why this is affecting me this way but it is. I am over my head. Way, way over my head. I'm probably not even his first bathroom-door affair. Maybe this very tie has been around another woman's wrists. I do not know what to do or say or how to be. I do not even know my own name half the time. I am not—

Liam squats in front of me, and the sight of his strong thighs and thick erection cuts off my rambling thoughts, and I struggle to gain my composure and recreate some version of Amy that is worthy of this man even if I, myself, am not.

His finger slides under my chin, and he levels my gaze with his. "I bought the condoms today for us, if that's what you're wondering. For us, Amy. I don't stockpile and have women in my hotel room ever night. I don't have women to my room, or let them inside my life, at all. Never. Just you."

He reads me like an open book I thought I'd shut years before. "Me," I whisper, reminded of his declaration that we are raw and honest or we are nothing.

"You," he agrees. "And us."

Us. I have never truly been a part of an "us", but the idea strokes a raw nerve ending, then caresses it with possibilities. I wet my suddenly dry lips and Liam leans in and brushes his mouth over mine before he murmurs, "And we need to get you to a doctor and on the pill."

"That takes weeks," I whisper, and the words vibrate with the same wistful quality I'd had earlier on the sidewalk, a wistfulness that I cannot seem to control any more than my feelings or reactions to Liam.

He cups my face and kisses me again, a soft brush of his mouth against mine, and I can feel myself sigh inside. This is what gets to me with Liam, the way he is so tender, and yet so dominating. It works for me. He works for me. So does the way he's trailing kisses over my jaw, teasing my neck, then my ear. "Until then," he voices, all velvet and seduction, "I'll be fantasizing about the moment the only thing wrapped around me is you."

My sex clenches with his words, slickness gathering on my bare thighs, and I decide right then that no woman knows what she has been missing until she has a man like Liam say such wicked things to her while he is naked in all his male perfection.

He leans back to study me, his blue stare probing, intimate. "Have you ever been bound before?"

I laugh and the sound is nervousness personified.

He doesn't laugh. His hands frame my face. "And you let me tie you up." It is a statement, not a question, and there is a husky rasp to his voice that tells me he is affected by this realization.

"Yes," I confirm, knowing somehow this is what he desires of me.

LISA RENEE JONES

His hand reaches behind me, cupping my backside, and he
pulls me to him. His shaft settles between my thighs, and I soften
instantly against him. "And I'm just barbaric enough to like the
idea of being the first of many things."

He's said something to this effect before. It's just as arousing
now as it was then. "You do seem to have a bit of a liking for the
word 'teacher'."

He caresses up my back and closes his hand on the back of
my head, pulling me to him, his cheek finding mine, his voice low,
raspy, as he murmurs, "I haven't even begun to start teaching you,
Amy. We have not even begun to go where I plan to take you."
He drags his lips over my jaw and his mouth lingers a breath from
mine. "You trusted me with your body by letting me bind you.
I'm going to make sure you don't regret it. That's step one, baby."

I do not know what he means by "step one", but his
seductive purr on the word "baby" does funny things to my chest
and his lips begin to trail over my jaw, teasing me with the
promise of a kiss that I hope soon will follow. And it does. His
mouth finds mine, a feather-light touch, a lick of his tongue, and I
moan with the barely there, teasing taste of him.

"I do like those little sounds you make," he murmurs,
rewarding me with another brush of his tongue against mine. I
moan again, unable to hold it back, ultra-sensitive to all this man
does to me. I'm relieved when he deepens the kiss, when he takes
me to that sweet spot where only he exists. This is what I want.
To be lost in him, and I arch into him, needing him closer,
craving that connection. Seeming to answer my plea, Liam inches
forward, leaning me against the door and cradling me more fully
on his lap, and his hands are all over me, teasing me, driving me
wild. The need to touch him spirals through me, and I tug at my
hands, but there is no escape. There is only the growing ache of
need inside me.

His lips leave mine, and I reach for his mouth, only to be
denied. "Untie me. I need to touch you."

130

He frames my face with his hands and I need them to be other places. Lots of other places. "You're not ready to be untied."

I laugh without humor. "Yes. Yes, I am."

"What are you thinking about right now?"

"I...I don't know."

"The first thing that comes into your head. Don't censor, just speak. Say it. Now. What are you thinking of now?"

"Your tattoo."

"Anything else?"

"Touching you."

"And?"

"Ripping the tie off my arms."

He lowers his forehead to mine and his hands brush my breasts, tease my nipples. "And now?"

"How much I don't want you to stop."

"That's the idea. Escape, baby. The lack of control is control. When you're hanging on each moment, anticipating what comes next, it leaves room for nothing else. That's what I want to do for you."

I think of his comment about sharks and the certainty there is more to his story than I know. "And who helps you escape, Liam?"

"We're going to the same place, Amy. I'm not standing outside watching." He dips his head low and his lips find my neck and then my ear. "I'm right here with you."

I squeeze my eyes shut, lavishing in the deep stroke of his hand down my back and the seductive reply of his words in my mind. Right here with you. That phrase shimmers down my spine and settles deep inside me. Liam is with me. In a tiny window of time, he has slipped past every wall I've erected.

"Look at me, Amy."

I pry my lashes open at his soft command and I feel a punch in my chest when my eyes meet his. I am going to fall hard for this man. I already have.

He leans in and kisses me, pressing my breasts together before dragging to tease my nipples, then dragging his mouth down my chin, to my neck and chest until his tongue laves one of my nipples, fulfilling a wish I so desired. I suck in a breath at the rough, wet heat suckling me, moving from one swollen tip to the next, mercilessly licking, nipping, teasing, and I can take no more.

"Liam, enough. Please. I need—"

"What I say you need," he finishes, his hands cupping my backside, lifting my belly to his mouth, dipping his tongue in my belly button, and then licking all the way to my hipbone. Nipping the sensitive flesh, licking again.

"Liam, damn it," I pant, and I never curse, but then I am never this undone. "You are making me insane."

He smiles against my belly. "That's the idea."

My quaking body disagrees. "No. No, it's not. Pleasure is the idea."

"Pleasure," he repeats, his eyes dancing with way too much male satisfaction for me to hope he's done tormenting me. "I thought that's what I was providing. Let's see. How about this?" He lowers his head and licks my clit, and I gasp, then whimper as he swirls his tongue around me several times, then teasingly asks, "Is that pleasure?"

I squeeze my thighs around his shoulders. "Stop tormenting me."

He blows on my clit. "It's called foreplay."

My lashes flutter but I manage to glare at him. "No, it's—"

His mouth closes down on me, and waves of pleasure ripple through me. I tug at my hands, desperate to hold his head, to make sure he doesn't stop this time. His fingers slide inside me, stretching me, caressing me. And his tongue, his amazing tongue, is both sandpaper and silk, stroking me to the edge, then masterfully soothing the ache. Over and over, he licks me to the shadow of bliss, and pulls it back.

"Liam," I gasp, unable to take it anymore. I am trembling with how close I am and how far at the same time. Needing him to give me relief, but he does not. His mouth leaves my clit and he slides up my body, shifting our hips and settling his cock thickly between my thighs, his searing stare meeting mine. "We come together," he says, and then presses inside me, stretching me, filling me, and I can barely breathe for the pleasure. I'd thought I'd wanted the sweet bliss his tongue had promised but in this moment, I know I did not. This is what I want. Together. He is where I need him but he does not move. He holds us there, his hands firmly on my hips, his shaft deep in my sex, and challenges me with, "What do you want, Amy?"

"Everything," I pant. "You. I want you."

His eyes darken, and he leans in, bringing our mouths a breath apart. "Everything?"

It is a question and a demand, and in this moment, perhaps in every moment since I met him, there is only one answer. "And more."

He does not move. We do not move. There is a spike of energy between us, a shift that I have never experienced, and do not understand, but it is like a wicked burn in my body, a craving unsatisfied. "More," he echoes a moment before he kisses me, and I taste the same burn in him, the same need. He molds me closer, arching into me, and begins to pump his hips. Time falls away. There is just the wild passion consuming us, and he is touching me, moving inside me, and I am going crazy with my hands tied. I want to touch him. I need to touch him.

He is on edge too, his grip tightening around my hips, his face buried in my neck, and with a guttural moan, he pushes harder, deeper, and my sex is one deep pulse around his shaft that begins a wave of pleasure and spreads through my entire body. I am there. I am falling, tumbling, and finally, I crash into that sweet spot. He pumps into me again, and I feel the shudder run through his body, or maybe it is me who is shuddering. I do not know how long it is before we melt into one another.

He reaches up and unties my hands and my arms fall around his neck. Liam shifts us and strokes the hair from my eyes. "We aren't anywhere near finished. You know that, right?"

"Promise?"

"Oh yeah. I promise. And I never make a promise I don't keep."

He shifts his weight and somehow stands up with me still wrapped around him, him still inside me. I bury my face in his neck, inhale the scent of him, the prickling of memories trying to surface fading into his words earlier tonight. Tell me who's scaring you and I promise you, Amy, I will make them go away. Or they will make him go away. I can't let that happen.

***

I wake to the morning light and the soft rumble of Liam's voice from someplace not far away, and I smile with the realization that I am naked and I did not have a nightmare last night. Thanks to Liam, I am certain who spent the night with his big body wrapped around mine. His big, sexy body, I amend. I am sated and relaxed. Safe. I feel safe with Liam.

Rolling over in the big, comfortable bed, I watch the curtain flutter over the sliding glass window only a few feet away, confirming Liam's location. "I'm not meeting with him today, Derek," I hear him say, sounding more than a little displeased. "Forget it. I have plans I'm not giving up for that jackass. Monday." A pause. "Yeah, well, he's lucky I'm motivated to stay around Denver for a few months. And no. That's none of your business."

Motivated to stay around Denver for a few months. I revel in these words, savoring them like I would fine wine in a bottle soon to be empty. But he will eventually return to New York, where you can never go again, I remind myself. Eventually he will be gone.

"Good morning."

My gaze lifts from the bed where it has fallen, to where he has parted the curtain and is standing in the opening of the door, dressed in nothing but a pair of blue pajama bottoms. I sit up, hugging the sheet to myself, but I am not shy in my inspection of his body, gobbling up every detail of this hot man I've had the pleasure of waking up to, from his lean, hard body to his lightly shadowed jaw line that only makes his goatee sexier. "You, Liam

Stone, are too good looking for the safety of womankind, and I probably look bad enough to scare small children and a few timid animals, too."

He laughs, and it is deep and wonderful and far better than sunshine or cinnamon rolls in the morning. He starts toward me and I hold up my hand. "No. Wait. Stay right there."

Stopping in his steps, his brow furrows, and I can't believe I'm about to do this, but that savor-him-until-he's-gone thing is ripe in my mind. Throwing aside the sheet, I expose my naked body, and I don't let the blast of heat from Liam's inspection slow me down. I rush forward and stand in front of him and I am as I was last night. Exposed in the most erotic of ways.

Liam arches a brow, a question in his gorgeous blue eyes I could drown in, and probably will before he goes back to New York. I answer his inquiry by dropping to my knees and pressing my mouth to his tattoo, my hands settling on his lean hips. He sucks in a breath, his body tensing ever so slightly, and I smile against a taut muscle. I have surprised him and this pleases me.

My gaze lifts to Liam's, and the heat I see in his stare only serves to empower me. I lick his stomach and drag my finger down the line of numbers until it dips beneath his waistband, a quick tease before it is gone. "Now," I say, "I am going to have to kiss my way down—"

A knock sounds on the door and Liam groans. I jump to my feet. "You have company?"

He wraps me in his arms. "Room service. I thought waking you up to breakfast in bed was a good thing until you started licking my tattoo."

"You were going to wake me up to breakfast in bed?"

"Then make you the second course." Another knock sounds and he gives me a quick kiss. "Just to be clear. Sexy is me waking up to you in my bed and looking just like you do now, tattoo licking optional, though not discouraged. Grab one of my shirts. I don't want any sneak peeks from room service. I plan to keep you for myself." He sets me aside and heads toward the other room.

I stare after him. He plans to keep me for himself. I fight the urge to call him back and make him seal those words with a promise.

Chapter Fourteen

Fifteen minutes later, I sit at a table on the balcony, drinking coffee and sampling an enormous amount of food Liam ordered to be sure I had something I liked to eat. What I like is him bare-chested and relaxed in his pajama bottoms, with sexy, mussed-up morning hair. And me, in his shirt, with his scent teasing my nostrils. I have never worn a man's shirt and that somehow makes wearing his shirt all the more intimate.

I pluck a grape from a basket with a variety of fruits and laugh as he argues his claim that the Fast & Furious movies are of cultural importance. "And you support this claim how?"

"The movies were released over the course of a decade. One could say they are a historical biography of the evolution of muscle cars."

"One such as you."

He smiles, and I swear his eyes are as perfect as the bright blue sky shadowing him. "One such as me."

I cover my now-empty plate that once held a fluffy cheese omelet. "Is there a collection of muscle cars to go along with this interest?"

"No muscle cars in my garage. Too impractical. I'll live vicariously through the movies."

"And here I thought you were a Bentley kind of guy."

"I'm not a flashy guy."

"But you love Fast & Furious."

"All men love Fast & Furious."

"But you are not all men, Liam."

His shoves his empty plate aside and leans close, his elbow on the table. "And why is that, Amy?"

"Oh, come on. You know you aren't like other guys. You're a prodigy, protégé, and billionaire."

"If I let those things become who I am, then they are all that I am. Judge me by who I am outside those things. Who would I be if those things were suddenly stripped away? A man who loves hamburgers, Fast & Furious, Thirty Seconds to Mars, and the History Channel, which we've determined we have in common."

I laugh at the way he sums himself up, charmed by his lack of arrogance and by the unexpected randomness of his interest. "And some violinist—"

"David Garrett."

"David Garrett," I repeat, "who you swear will seduce me into loving his music. All these pieces of you are not what I expected."

"Is that good?" His voice is softer now, rougher.

"Yes. Yes, it's good."

"Unexpected and good. Much like us."

I suck in a breath, surprised, pleased, warmed by this man in a way the morning sunshine cannot begin to touch. "Yes," I say, sealing my decision to weed through all the history I have to hide, to have just a few weeks with this man. "Unexpected." So very unexpected.

"And good," he prods.

I smile. "And good."

His cell phone rings. He grimaces and hits decline, glancing at me and answering my unasked question. "Derek, the guy I was talking to when you woke up. He's an investor in the building project and the only reason I entertained the idea of being involved. He gets me and what I do."

"Do you need to go meet with him? Because I'm fine if you do."

"No. They'll wait until tomorrow." He changes the subject. "Do you have a passport?"

My unease is instant; a fizzle of fear over his motives sparks into life. I laugh nervously, feeling as if I have been on a casual fun drive and just got sideswiped. "My travels have been as ambitious as sampling the various cupcake shops around Manhattan."

He smiles, and it is as devastatingly sexy as his tattoo. Well, almost. "Sweet tooth?"

"Mammoth-sized, though I don't indulge often or I'll be mammoth-sized." I sound halfway okay, I think, but all I can think is why did he ask about the passport?

He lifts the cover of a plate to display some sort of gooey chocolate waffle concoction. "I do, too." He hands me a fork. "I'll dare if you will."

I take a fork and my hand trembles. Liam gently shackles my wrist and I inhale and look at him. "What's wrong, Amy?"

I want to scream at my complete inability to mask my emotions with this man. I've always handled myself smoothly. Okay, well, after that first year of melting down. "I feel like I'm keeping you from work." Lie. Lie. Lie. You are such a liar.

His eyes narrow and I swear he knows what I am, if not who I am. I think he will call me on my reply, but he does not. His hand slides away and he motions to the chocolate goo on the plate. "Shall we?"

"Yes," I breathe out, and I want to know why he asked about a passport—but at this point, it would be too obvious a question and invite more from him. I spoon up the sugary treat and take a bite.

Liam does the same, watching me as he tastes the dessert-like breakfast item. "Good?"

"Yes. Delicious."

"Now we have two things on our to-do list," he says, referencing my confession about list making I'd shared while avoiding other personal things, like my dead family, both the fake one and the real one.

"Two things?"

"The doctor," he reminds me, and when I should be worried about the passport reference that seems so bizarre, I instead remember last night. Until then, I'll be fantasizing about the moment the only thing wrapped around me is you.

Somehow, I am now both warm and cold at the same time. "And the second to-do item?"

"David Garrett is touring in Europe the rest of the year. That's why I asked about the passport. I'd like to take to you to a concert." His lips quirk in that sexy way they do. "He'll seduce you with his music and I'll seduce you in another country."

Tension uncurls inside me, replaced by regret. Not only did he not have bad intentions, he had romantic ones I don't know if I can accept without taking the risk that my identity would be scrutinized. "As much as I would like to go, my job is only certain for a few months. I need to look for something more long-term."

His expression doesn't change, but I sense a sharp shift in his mood, a heaviness in the air around us that wasn't there seconds before. "The boss who provided you with an apartment."

I bristle, something in his tone setting me on edge. "What does that mean, Liam?"

"It's not safe to go to work for a guy you don't know and who provides you with an apartment. Does he have access to it?"

My pulse races at the concern that mimics my own. "It's my apartment. He just arranged it with a realtor. I have to pay for it."

He studies me and the seconds feel eternal before he says, "There is something about the situation that feels wrong. I'm going to have him checked out."

I assume he is talking about my boss not the realtor, but either way, this is exactly what I have feared. The more involved I am with Liam, the more he will dig into my life. "He's just my boss. And only for a few months. That's the point. I need to focus on finding another job that is more long-term. This is a bridge job."

"That friend of mine, Derek. He runs a large real estate investment firm. I'll introduce you and see if he might have anything you might be interested in."

I am not about to apply for work with his friend, who then would have a human resources file on me, but I can't say that. "Thank you."

"And I'm going to pay your rent for a year tomorrow so you don't have to stress about it anymore."

I am stunned and angry all in one blow. And hurt. I feel again like a charity case bordering on becoming a tramp. "No. You are not." I shove to my feet. "I'm going to get dressed and leave."

I barely manage to slide out of my seat before he's in front of me and his hand is on my arm, possessiveness in the action that I crave and reject. Feeling vulnerable, I lash out. "I guess I pay you for my rent by fucking you all night until we both can't walk?" I can't even believe I can talk like this. I can't believe I let myself be in this situation.

Liam looks stunned. "Where did that come from, Amy?"

"I'm not some 'kept woman', Liam. You've got the wrong girl."

"Kept woman? That's crazy." He softens his voice. "You have to know that's not how I am or how we are."

"How can I not feel like that? I like how I feel when I'm with you, Liam. I do. Or I did. Except right now. I don't like how I feel right now. I don't want your money, Liam."

"It's not about money..."

It's not about the money. I hear nothing else. Spots form in front of my eyes, and a distant, unwelcome memory forces itself on me. I squeeze my eyes shut, trying to block what I instinctively do not want to see, but it's too late. The past refuses to be ignored and I am transported back to Texas, to a day when I am excitedly running up the stairs of my family home to share my acceptance letter from the University of Texas with my mother. I can see the blue jean skirt and red tank top I am wearing, and the smell of the honeysuckle bushes off the side of our huge wooden porch is ripe in my nostrils. I reach for the doorknob to open it and freeze at the sound of my mother shouting. It isn't about the money. It was never about money.

"Amy."

I blink and realize that I am on the bed with Liam sitting beside me, his hand on my leg, and I do not remember how I got here. "I, ah…"

"Blacked out," he says. "You scared the fuck out of me."

"I'm sorry. I…" I sit up and lean against the headboard. "I'm okay." It's not about the money. I hear my mother's voice in my head again and drop my face to my hand. Desperately at times, I have tried to remember my mother's voice, to hear my mother's voice, to remember the way she used to run around the house singing to the radio. But not today, not in this partially formed memory some part of me seems to be clawing to get at while another blocks it from entry. Maybe it isn't even real. Sometimes I don't know what is or isn't anymore. I do not know how I can want to know the truth and fear it this badly.

Liam's hand settles on the side of my head and he presses his cheek to mine. "You're okay, baby. I'm here and nothing is going to happen to you." My hand goes to his, and I want to tell him it's not me I'm worried about. It's him. He strokes my hair and leans back, gently turning my face to his. "Can you walk to the car?"

The dull throb in my forehead is easing, but I must not be clearheaded because I truly have no idea what he's talking about. "Car? Where are we going?"

"We need to go to the ER and make sure you're okay."

I stiffen and fight through the clawing sensation in my gut, the aftermath of hearing my mother's voice. "No. No ER. It's cluster headaches. They feel eternal but they only last a few minutes."

"How often?"

"They went away several years ago and just started again."

"Have you had an MRI?"

"Yes. I'm fine. They usually can't explain why they happen to sufferers. They just happen. I'm supposed to watch for triggers like stress, change of environment, and what I eat. I'm sure it's the move."

"Do you take meds?"

"There isn't much they can do for them since they come fast and hard. Acupuncture helped. They went away for years after I tried it."

"And they just came back today?"

"A couple of days ago."

His hands curve around my calves and he scoots closer. "Nightmares and cluster headaches. I'm not going to ask all the questions that come to mind. Not now, but sometime soon you're going to have to tell me. You know that, right?"

All too well, I think. "Moving here was a big decision, Liam. I've always been like this. Big things mess with me. It goes way back to my childhood Godzilla nightmares."

"I'll take that answer for now as long as you agree to see a doctor."

"I don't need a doctor."

"What if you'd been driving?"

"I wasn't."

"Or walking down the stairs. I'm going to be stubborn on this. You need to see a doctor."

"Acupuncture is what worked before. I'll find a place to go."

"I think you should be checked out by a real doctor again to be safe."

"I'm not spending thousands of dollars for them to run MRIs and tests to tell me what I already know."

"Humor me and see someone. I'll pay for it."

"Stop trying to spend money on me."

"Stop hyper-focusing on the money. This isn't about—"

My head pinches. "Stop. Stop. Don't say it again. I get it. You have money and you spend $100 bills like it's my penny. But I am not wasting it, no matter how much of it you have. I know what works and that's acupuncture." And it does. It's how I'd recovered years before.

Disapproval furrows his brow. "I'll get you an appointment, but if it doesn't work—"

"It will and I can get my own appointment."

"But you won't because you want to save money, which is exactly why I'm going to take some of the pressure off of you. Tomorrow I'm going to the leasing office and paying your rent for a year, and—"

"No, I told you. I'm not going to take your money."

"It's done, baby. No strings attached. No conditions. If you want to ask for a refund after I pay it, you can donate the money to charity, but I won't take it back. A gift is a gift and I expect nothing in return. Not even a promise of tomorrow." He leans in and kisses me, and I mean to pull back but his tongue presses past my teeth for one irresistible, deep, silky caress, before he adds, "And tomorrow won't be enough."

"Liam—"

He gives me another quick kiss and I lose my thought. "Stop kissing me," I reprimand, sounding completely unconvincing. "You're trying to distract me."

"Is it working?"

"Yes. That's the problem."

"Then why would I stop?" he queries, looking exceedingly pleased with himself. He leans in for yet another kiss.

I press my fingers to his lips. "No. Not again. I remember what I was saying. Please stop throwing money at me."

He covers my fingers with his hand. "I want to do this for you, Amy." His voice softens, turning gravelly. "Please let me."

Please let him? My heart squeezes with the sincerity I sense in him and I reach up and stroke his cheek, then trace the line of his goatee. He is amazing and generous and so much more than I bargained for in every possible way. "You're new territory to me, Liam. I have never met anyone like you. You're overbearingly generous and overwhelmingly male, or maybe it's the reverse. Sometimes I don't know how to respond."

He pulls me down on the bed and under him. "I'd say I'd show you, but I think we better wait until later considering you blacked out on me a few minutes ago."

"I told you. I know what is wrong. It's over. I'm fine. Show me."

"Your sure?"

Finally, a question I can answer without hesitation. "Yes. Please." Please take me away and block a piece of my past that is clawing its way through me.

***

It's nearly one in the afternoon, and Liam and I are walking through the hotel lobby, our fingers laced together. I am such a nervous wreck I do not even care that wearing the same dress as the night before screams "sleepover" to the hotel staff. I cannot walk away from memories that hold answers, but at the same time my mind rejects even thinking about what that means right now. Not when Liam and I are heading to my apartment so I can change clothes before we go to the cellular store and pick up my ID, which is just another chance for Liam to find out it's a Colorado license. Before I deal with that potential bombshell, I have to explain why my things I left in New York City haven't been delivered. I hate lying, but I hate the idea of Liam being put in danger far more. I just want it over with, but a voice in my head quickly whispers, Lies breed lies. But questions breed questions, and when I made the decision to stay with Liam, I made the decision, like it or not, to own being Amy Bensen with him.

Liam and I step beyond the awning of the hotel exit and into the beaming sunlight. I cast his profile an inspection, and my breath hitches at how exquisitely male he is, his thick, dark hair a finger-combed sexy mess. He's dressed in a snug black polo pullover, black jeans, and some kind of deck shoes. Half an hour ago, he was exquisite in nothing but droplets of water and the soap that I had the pleasure of lathering him with. I have never showered with a man. I have never felt like this about anyone. I don't know what "this" is, except that it's intense in all the right ways and I don't want my past to destroy it before it ever takes form, as it has every other relationship I've had in my life.

We pause at the curb to allow cars to pass before we cross the street to my apartment and I steal a glimpse of Liam to discover him doing the same to me. He smiles a devastatingly sexy smile at me, and pulls me under his arm, melding our hips together. My arm slides around his waist and he leans down and gives me a quick peck on the lips. A sweet, hot spot forms in my chest. It is this moment that speaks to me in a way all the hot sex we've had last night and this morning cannot. He doesn't do relationships. I don't do relationships, and yet that is exactly what it feels like we are doing.

We cross the street without breaking apart, and I have this sense of being sheltered from the storm brewing all around me. At the apartment elevator, Liam doesn't seem keen on letting me go, and we huddle in the car, still holding onto each other. I think of the leasing office providing me instructions for my work assignments and a needling begins inside me. Why exactly would my handler leave anything with anyone for me?

Approaching my apartment door, I dig for my key, and will my nerves to calm down. The "zone" my fake self slides into to perform seems to be pretty much non-existent where Liam is concerned, and I have to find it now. For his own good.

Somehow, I unlock the door with a steady hand. The walls I erect while inside my zone are trying to form, but they are as paper-thin as my ability to resist this man. Entering the hallway, Liam is on my heels, but I pause in front of him, and I flip on the light, stalling to inhale a deep breath before letting him follow me forward. I turn to wait on him to shut the door, blocking his entry, a soldier drawing a hard line.

He arches a brow and I really wish he wasn't so damn sexy when he did that. "Don't jump to conclusions," I warn. "The moving company lost my things. I'm filing a claim. I took out the insurance I needed so I'll have my things replaced, so don't go offering to help. I don't need help."

"It could take weeks to get a check."

"I bought some things to get me by today."

He stares down at me with that unreadable mask he wears like a champion poker player, and then grabs my hand and says, "Show me."

"Show you what?"

146

"Exactly what you have to survive on the next few weeks until you get a check." He doesn't give me time to argue, dragging me with him to the bedroom, and straight to my closet.

I cringe when he opens the door to the empty room and then actually glares at me as if I've done something wrong. "What exactly is it that you bought to get you by?"

"It's not your business to—"

"I'm making it my business." He releases my hand and walks to the dresser, opening several empty drawers and removing the limited items I purchased yesterday, setting them all on the bed. "This is what you call getting by?" He looks at a price tag and grimaces. "A couple of outfits from the bargain racks and not much else?"

My defenses prickle. "I'm not spending money I don't have to."

He grabs me and sits down on the bed, leading me between his legs, his fingers playing on my hips, his mouth pressing to my belly. It's so unexpected that my mood softens instantly and I almost forget how overbearing he is being. "Change clothes and let's get out of here," he says softly. "I don't like this apartment or you in it."

My suspicion over him not pushing me on the purchase of more clothing takes a backseat to his concern over my living arrangements. "What's wrong with this place and me in it?"

"Aside from me preferring you in my hotel and my bed, I don't like the premise of a boss you've never met arranging your lease."

He is turning the pages on my cover story far too quickly. "Lots of employers line up housing when employees relocate."

"Not for an employee they don't intend to keep for more than a few months."

"My ex-boss is good friends with him and all he did was contact his realtor to find me something."

"Are you certain he's not on the lease and has no access to the apartment?"

He hits a nerve that is already open. "Of course he doesn't have access."

"Nevertheless, I'm going to get your locks changed."

"You can't just decide to change my locks, Liam," I say, despite that being exactly what I intend to do. I have to reel him in before he dials into things that get him into trouble. "And you can't just take over my life."

"I'm not asking for a key."

"No. You'd just take one. And this isn't about a key. It's about you being assuming and bossy."

His hands slide under my dress, up the back of my thighs. "You like those things."

"Sometimes." Often. Too often. I fear it speaks of just how much I'm breaking down again. "And those times usually include us not wearing clothing."

"Just stay with me at the hotel. Problem solved."

My desire to escape to his world and block out my own is so intense it's frightening. Too easily he could leave and I will be broken and alone again. "I need to stay here and start making this home."

"I have room service, which lets us stay in bed longer and more often."

A knock sounds on the door and I tense before I can stop myself. "Expecting someone?" Liam asks.

"I don't know anyone to expect," I tell him and my mind races. Who would visit me except maybe my handler? And I haven't even checked the email I was given. The very idea that I've missed something important sets my heart leapfrogging. I flash back to the call in the hospital. They're coming for you. If they come for me, they could come for Liam too.

Chapter Fifteen

I twist out of Liam's arms and rush for the hallway, certain he will follow. Eager to get as much of a jumpstart on him as I can, I all but sprint the rest of the distance and a second knock sounds on the door right as I reach for the knob. I don't bother with "who is it?" as I normally would. I yank the door open and I am both stunned and relieved to find Jared leaning casually on the doorframe, one elbow on the frame above his head, a Boeing logo on his pale blue t-shirt.

He straightens when he sees me, one thin strand of light brown hair falling from the clasp at the back of his neck. "Hey," he says, and offers me a sexy smile I imagine a guy like him has down to a science.

That familiar sensation I get with him is back. "Hi."

He pulls an envelope from behind his back and the adrenaline already racing through me spikes. "This blew off of your door so I thought I'd hold onto it for you," he explains, and offers it to me.

Remarkably, my hand does not shake as I accept it, and I note that it's free of any text or stickers. It's also not sealed. "I appreciate you doing this."

"It gave me an excuse to check on you." He gives me a half-smile I just manage to return as he adds, "You gave me a scare yesterday. I actually came by last night before the envelope to check on you but you didn't answer. I was concerned about you being alone after you almost bit the dust."

"She wasn't alone. She was with me, and what do you mean she almost bit the dust?"

Liam steps by my side, his hand sliding around my waist, and the touch is a branding, his hip leaning into mine, fingers flexing into my skin. The two men's gazes lock and I am suddenly swimming in a pool of testosterone, in need of a life raft. The crackle of power being pulled and pushed is almost palpable. The certainty Liam and I will have words over the encounter: absolute. He's out of control, or rather, he's making me out of control.

"Liam Stone," I say, "meet Jared Ryan. Jared lives across the hall, or at least he will for thirty days."

"Thirty days?"

"That's right," Jared says, offering no explanation, the two-word answer hanging in the air with the heaviness of a storm cloud about to erupt. Silence lingers and we all three just stand there. And stand there. Oh good grief, I'm losing my mind. Someone say something!

"Do you work for Boeing?" Liam asks, proving he is not done being direct, and I am not done being flustered by it, and yet, I find myself curious about the answer as well.

"No," Jared replies. "But I have a Dallas Cowboys shirt too and I don't play football."

"Smartass," Liam says, sounding irritated while I am slightly amused, though still uncomfortably lost in the power play between these two. I wonder why Jared is so secretive. Maybe it's simply that he doesn't like Liam. I'm pretty sure Liam doesn't like him either. Maybe though, like me, Jared has something to hide. This, with the familiarity I feel for him, does not sit well.

"Most of the time," Jared agrees, and I find myself caught in the line of his stare. "Glad you're okay. If you need anything, you know where to find me." He turns away and makes his way to his door and neither Liam nor I move, and I wonder if Liam is as surprised by Jared's abrupt departure as I am.

Jared unlocks his door and he's about to enter when he cuts us a sideways look. "I'm in safe now. You two can go back inside."

He disappears into his apartment, leaving me with my new envelope and the overwhelming man that is Liam Stone.

I am the first to move from the doorway, turning away from Liam with every intention of escaping to the other room to see what is in the envelope. I cannot be cornered by Liam until I know what I am facing. In another mad dash, the bedroom is my destination, but I do not make it. Liam shackles my arm and the next thing I know I am back against the wall, caged in his arms. Clearly, we are turning the entryway into the confrontation corner of the apartment. "What does he mean you almost bit the dust?" he demands.

"I hadn't eaten." Truth.

"You had another blackout."

"You're being overbearing." Another truth. I'm liking this confrontation so far. I'd like it better if it were after I opened the envelope.

"Don't be coy," he warns.

I deflect. "What was the 'she's with me' thing? I'm not property, Liam." I try to duck under his arm. He blocks me and I can feel emotions building inside me, ready to explode. I need to know what is in this envelope. "Let me pass. You're being more barbaric than you are Prince Charming." I can't pull it back. It's out and it's like a rock landing at our feet and I try to cover it up. "You're suffocating me. I need space."

It's too late. Liam's hands drop away as if I've burned him and there is no missing the petrified look on his face. My gut twists in knots. "Stop looking like one of your sharks just bit you."

I head to the bedroom and this time he lets me. He lets me. Damn it, I keep turning this into more than it is but he sends mixed signals. I don't need or want Prince Charming. Okay, maybe sometimes I do. I don't know anything anymore.

I pause at the bed to grab my shorts and t-shirt I wore yesterday, and I both wish Liam would appear and pray he will not. Yep. That is how much of a tripped-out mess I am. And I lied again. I said I wasn't looking for Prince Charming, but deep down, I know I've made Liam my hero. And I know how dangerous that is, for too many reasons to count.

Glancing at the still-empty doorway, I head to the bathroom and shut myself inside, setting the envelope down on the sink and staring at it like it's alive and will move. The possibility it might send me racing for another new location is too much to take. I can't seem to make myself open it. I kick off my heels and tear my dress over my head, then stare at the envelope some more. It still hasn't moved and I still haven't opened it.

"Just get it over with, Amy," I whisper and reach for it, flipping open the flap and pulling out what appears to be a copy of my signed lease with a note attached. I was in your neighborhood and Dermit wanted me to check on you and drop this by. Looks like I missed you. Call the office if you need anything. Luke Evernight. I should be relieved—this is not a warning or instructions to leave—but instead a frisson of unease slides down my spine and I'm not sure why. What is it that is bothering me?

Abruptly the door behind me opens, and Liam is an unstoppable force. He lifts me and sets me on the counter, dislodging the papers from my hand in the process, and sending them flying to the floor. His arms frame mine, his hands on the surface by my knees.

"Reality check, Amy. I never promised to be Prince Charming."

I flinch. "I told you. I'm not looking for a Prince Charming."

"I fuck and move on."

"You told me that, too. Stop saying it. I don't want to hear it."

"The last time I had a long-term girlfriend was college, and she left me because she said I was self-centered, cold, and just wanted between her legs. And it was true. For all kinds of reasons, it was true. I am not a relationship guy."

"What do you want me to say, Liam? Please fuck me for a few days and move on? I didn't even say that word before I met you. But fine, fine, fine! Fuck me for a few days and move on, but stay out of my business. Stop asking questions. Stop trying to change my locks and order me to go to the doctor and just stop. No barbarian routine unless it's when we are naked. Period. The end."

He scrubs a hand through his hair. "You don't get it. I'm not explaining myself well, which is a testament to how out of my skin you make me. My point is that I'm the one who's on unfamiliar territory. When I saw your smartass neighbor look at you like he wanted to strip you naked, I had to fight the urge to throttle him. I have never felt that. Never."

"What? No. He—no."

"He wants you. I want you. I can't walk away from you, Amy, and I have this sense that you could bolt at any minute. And yes, you're right. I'm being barbaric. And intense. That's who I am and I can't be anyone but me. When I want something, I go after it. And baby, I want you, and all I can say is you might be smart to run before I get any more into you, but please don't."

His voice is gruff, affected, vulnerable in a way I didn't know him capable of being. And his eyes, those deep blue, amazing eyes are blurred with shadows and torment over me, over something in his past I am not sure I understand. All I know is he's letting me see it, and him, and he is exactly what he preaches. Raw and honest, and intense, and I believe in this moment we are a rainbow of the same colors, none of them bright or beautiful. We are the many shades of gray and black, hoping to find a glimmer of light in each other, not more darkness.

I press my hand to his cheek and he leans into my touch. "I don't want to go anywhere," I whisper, and I don't want him to go anywhere either, but deep down I know he will or I will. We are destined to end. This is the way of my world and he is as captive to it as I am without knowing it.

"Then I'm not going to let you," he says, his hand sliding into my hair, his mouth closing down on mine, and there is more than passion that bleeds into my mouth. There is the promise he means to hold onto me, and I pray it's not one we will both regret.

***

Liam and I are about to walk into the cell phone store when Liam's phone rings. "It's Derek. I'll meet you inside." Relief washes over me. He won't see my Colorado license.

Liam holds the door for me and I step into the store and hear him say, "No, I am not going to meet with him today," followed by a deliciously deep, sexy laugh I could seriously get drunk on.

I find Scott behind the counter on the phone and he waves me forward. Eager to take advantage of Liam's absence and wondering how long I can really keep secrets from him, I rush forward. Rushing does me no good. The customer Scott is talking to is difficult, and I find myself twisting my fingers in knots, trying to will the call the end. My gaze falls on a typed note about some cell phone accessories and my mind goes to the typed note left on my door. I can picture it.

I was in your neighborhood and Dermit wanted me to check on you and drop this by. Looks like I missed you. Call the office if you need anything. Luke Evernight.

I straighten and stiffen. The note was typed, but it sounded like he'd handwritten it when I didn't answer the door. That isn't logical. Why didn't he handwrite it? Surely he didn't go back to his office to type it. And why would he type a note stating I wasn't home before discovering that to be the case?

Scott hangs up and slides my ID to me. "Here you go, Ms. Bensen. Nice and safe."

I shake off enough of the unease to focus on the present. "Thank you. I'm so glad you kept calling. I thought it was a wrong number."

He frowns. "I only called the one time and got lucky you answered."

"One time?"

He nods.

"Oh." My throat thickens. Someone else had called me. "I received another 'unknown' call. Can you look up who it came from?"

"Unknown or blocked?"

I grab my phone and look. "Oh," I say again. "Blocked. I guess I thought they were the same. Yours was blocked, too."

"No, blocked means you intentionally make sure the person can't find your contact info. I called from my cell so I blocked the call."

"But no one but you has my number." And Meg, but not before the first call in question.

"It's probably overflow from whoever had the number before you."

"Okay. Thank you for everything." I sound robotic. I don't feel it. I feel more like a wheel spinning out of control. Liam's right. Something is off about what is happening around me. I pull up the internet on my phone and go into Gmail, watching the door for Liam, and checking my new inbox. Nothing. No messages from my "boss", or anyone for that matter. Suddenly, that apartment I will never call mine by choice feels creepy. I'm all for going to Liam's safe hotel. I'll figure out what to do next when Liam goes to his meetings tomorrow.

I reach the exit and Liam holds the door for me, ending a call as he does, and just seeing him brings down my nerves a notch. We start walking toward both the hotel and my apartment. "I found an acupuncturist to come to the hotel this afternoon and do a treatment," he informs me.

"I didn't even know they would work on Sundays, let alone do house calls."

He winks. "I can be persuasive."

"You have to stop spending money on me."

"Stop thinking of everything like it's money spent. I know that's hard. I had to adjust at one point. This is who I am, Amy. You have to get used to it."

Get used to it. I want the chance to get used to him, not the money.

"I say," Liam continues, "we order room service, watch movies, and get naked so I can be barbaric in approved territory.

155

Actually I think I'll call that side of me 'the beast'. Let's go set him free."

"The beast?" I laugh, and I like that he is confident enough to laugh at himself, and try to find boundaries that work for us both. "The beast?"

"That's right, baby. Let's go get your things from your apartment."

My fear of being attached to him and then losing him comes back with a force. Once I move to his hotel indefinitely, I'll never want to leave. I stop dead in my tracks and turn to him. "Liam." We stand there in the middle of the sidewalk, forcing several people to walk around us. "I like that side of you. I like you."

He pulls me hard against him. "I'm insane for you, Amy. 'Like' lasted all of ten minutes."

"I've been alone a long time," I admit, and I embrace being honest. I let myself be vulnerable now for fear of being destroyed later. "I'm afraid of forgetting how to be without you." I laugh nervously. "I can't believe I'm telling you this in the middle of a busy sidewalk."

He pulls me out of the crowd, settling my back against a brick wall, his big body shielding me from the outside. "How long, Amy?"

"Six years." It's out before I ever even process my documented story.

He curses and scrubs his face. "Since you were eighteen."

I nod. "Yes."

"Without anyone else to depend on?"

"Right."

"Did you date?"

"I tried in college. My dorm mate's legs ended up around my boyfriend's neck and I was done with the dating thing."

"No wonder you have nightmares and cluster headaches."

"They aren't headaches." I don't mean to blurt it out, but it feels good to tell him. To feel safe enough to let him into a small part of what the battle I'm fighting. "That's a lie I tell so people won't think I'm some sort of crazy person. They're blackouts and flashbacks."

He kisses me. "That's not a lie, baby. It's survival."

He's right. Surviving is all I've lived for. Until now. Until him.

"How?"

I don't have to ask what he means. I've implied I lost my family all at once. I've promised myself I will lie to protect him. To ensure he survives, but not now. "I can't talk about it without crumbling." My eyes prickle, the pain of the past biting a path through my body, into my heart, deep into my soul. "I...I can't."

He wraps his arm around my neck and lowers his forehead to mine, and if I felt sheltered before, I feel completely protected now, like nothing exists but Liam. "I've had my share of dark days," he confesses. "I get it. You don't have to do or say anything you don't want to."

I surprise me—and probably him—by laughing, and he leans back to look at me. "I don't have to do anything I don't want to accept," I amend, "change my locks, go to the doctor, and let you spend money on me I don't want you to spend."

He smiles, and it is a devastatingly sexy smile. "Exactly. Except those things." He motions me forward. "Let's go get your things and go lock ourselves in the hotel room."

Chapter Sixteen

I wake the next morning to the sound of a cell phone ringing, and I am naked, on my stomach, and Liam's heavy leg is draped over mine. Liam groans and opens his eyes. "If I ignore it, it will end."

I laugh. "But it will ring again, and don't you have meetings?"

"The alarm hasn't gone off. I'm not leaving this bed with you one second before I have to." The cell stops ringing and the alarm goes off. He groans again. "I think I'll call in sick." The cell starts ringing again. "Oh, well hell." He rolls over and answers the call. "What do you mean he's not here?" He moves to lean on the headboard and I lift up on my elbows, my gaze riveted by the tattoo. That sexy, wonderful tattoo I could happily wake up to every morning.

"Emergency my ass," Liam continues. "This is a power play of some sort. Oh, come on. You know it is. And no, I'm not coming in until he's back. That's the intention. Get me committed to the project and I'll do it his way. I won't. Meeting with anyone else before he and I come to terms is a waste of everyone's time."

I can't help myself. I inch over to Liam and begin kissing his stomach. Liam glances down at me, his eyes simmering with heat and the sheet begins to lift. I laugh and lick the 3.14 numbers above the "pi" sign.

"I'm staying and not because of him," Liam tells Derek, or I assume it's Derek. "Call me when he gets back. We'll go from there." He ends the call, tosses the phone, and drags me up his body before rolling me to my back.

"Oh, the things I can do to you with a full day in bed." It's a wicked warning and a promise of punishment in the most pleasurable of ways. He proved this to me last night. He'll torment me. He'll take me to the edge and make me wait. He'll make me ask for things I never thought I could ask for. But he will make me forget everything but him. And right now, I need that more than answers. I need him.

***

Mid-afternoon finds Liam and me downtown at a high-rise building on the top floor, snuggled into the cozy chairs of a coffee shop that overlooks the site where the new shopping complex is supposed to be located. I'm dressed in a pair of black shorts and a pink tank Liam has forced me to buy by dragging me in a store, slapping down a card, and telling me to spend a ridiculous figure or he'd spend it for me. I still can't believe he did it—or that I ultimately let him.

I study him now, removing things from a sleek leather briefcase, dressed in a casual pair of dark blue jeans and a snug blue pullover that makes his eyes inhumanly blue. He begins to pull his drafting pad out of a slim case, and in an act I'm finding familiar, he runs his fingers over his goatee. My gaze falls on a watch he's wearing that I have not seen until today. It has a thick silver band and a brand that probably means it costs as much as some people's houses.

He glances up to catch me watching him, leaning in to give me a quick, hot brush of his lips against mine. He then offers me my computer from inside his bag. "Thank you," I say, accepting it, wishing I didn't have to think about the reason I have it.

"What exactly are you working on?"

"Property listings. Boring stuff."

"And what did you do in New York?"

"Research and admin work. Boring."

"What kind of research?"

I hate this. I hate it so much. I just want to tell him everything. "It really depended on what my boss had going on. Nothing as exciting as pyramids. I wish."

"You like history."

"History that is a mystery."

"Like the pyramids."

This is a connection to my past. I should change the subject. I don't. "Yes. Like the pyramids."

"Why a history teacher and not an archeologist?"

"I did what felt right at the time."

"After you lost your family."

"Yes. I went on to college, but...I just went through the motions. By the time I woke up it felt like I just needed my degree and a higher income." I shake off what could turn into a flashback and more information than I should tell him. "Tell me about your plans for the building. What are you drafting today?"

"I'm going to do the underground tunnels from the pyramid to the various other buildings."

"Like the real ones."

"Exactly. And glass blocks will create the actual pyramid." He flips his design around for me to see. "I was thinking about a-hole's argument that pyramids have been done, and he's right. They have. But I have this idea to design two pyramids on top of the main structure. It's never been done."

"I can't picture it."

He quickly sketches a small drawing, simple, but enough for me to understand. "Like you're stacking the pyramids. Can that actually work? It seems unstable."

"They won't be stacked. They'll be structures within structures."

"I'm intrigued. I can't wait to see it. I hope you build it."

"If that doesn't win over a-hole, then I'll take it somewhere else and build it. Then you can see it. Maybe we can go see the real pyramids together."

Like I am going to be around no matter where he is, and when he builds it, and to travel with him. Maybe I should be worried that he is so invested in me in such a short window of time, but I am not. I feel the connection between us and I do not believe it is something anyone could fake. And maybe I should worry that he is so interested in something connected to my past, but again, I'm just not. Right or wrong, I trust Liam and I am hungry for every moment I have with him. I want to find a way to make it last.

I smile. "So you can seduce me in a pyramid?"

He laughs. "That sounds worth the trip, don't you think?"

My cell phone rings and I stiffen, my playful mood evaporating instantly.

Liam picks my phone up from the table between us where I've set it and slides it into my hand. "I'm right here, you know," he says, reminding me that he remembers all too well how I'd freaked out over a phone call the night before.

And it's comforting. He's right here. I am not alone. I glance at the number and feel my shoulders visibly relax. "Meg," I say. "You met her at the restaurant." Liam visibly relaxes as well, settling back in his chair and I answer the call. "Hi, Meg."

"Hi, Amy. Did you get the executed lease Luke dropped by?"

My unease is instant. "Yes. I got it. Tell him thank you."

"And you're doing fine? He said Mr. Williams wanted to be sure."

"Yes. I am, but I have some questions. Would you have a number for Mr. Williams?"

There is a moment of silence. "No. No number." She lowers her voice. "Luke is weird with Dermit Williams. Apparently the guy is loaded and Luke doesn't trust me enough with his info."

"Can you ask Luke to call me?"

"Sure. He's out of town again, though. I swear I am going to go nuts in this office alone. How about happy hour?"

I glance at Liam, and find his head buried in his drafting pad, his brows dipped in deep thought, and I want nothing more than to hang up the phone and get lost in watching him create his masterpiece. "Not tonight." But I know she holds a key to my new boss. "Soon. Maybe tomorrow. I'll call you then, if that works?"

"Sure. Call me."

"And you'll have Luke call me?"

"When he gets back into town."

"Which will be when?"

"Next week."

Next week? "If he calls in can you ask him for Mr. Williams' number?"

"I'll see what mood he's in."

I sigh. "Okay. Thanks."

I hang up the call and set my phone down and Liam glances up at me. "Who are Luke and Mr. Williams?"

"And here I thought you were lost in your work."

"I can multitask. I think you know that."

I blush at his reference to the many naughty things he did to me the night before and this morning. "Luke is the realtor and Mr. Williams is my boss."

"Who you can't reach?"

"He's out of the country."

He narrows his gaze on me. "Everything okay, Amy?"

And I know it's a prod for me to share more with him, but I care too much for Liam to be any more selfish than I already have. "Yes," I say, and if my life wasn't a big circus and I didn't have this gnawing sensation that I'm about to turn his life into one too, it would be.

He takes my hand and pulls me to him. "Make a doctor's appointment. I want to be as naked inside you as you make me feel. As I want you to trust me enough to be with me."

It is the most erotic, seductive thing anyone has ever said to me. "I do trust you."

And I see in his face that he believes this is a lie when it is the truth. It's not about trust. It's about danger.

***

The real world crashes down on me when I wake up Wednesday morning and the "a-hole" investor returns and Liam

162

has to go to work. Having showered and dressed before Liam, at his urging and insistence—he would not make his meeting if I was still in bed where he wanted to be with me—I sit at the dining table of the hotel suite, coffee in hand, wishing the clawing sensation in my gut would go away. Having Liam to myself these past few days has been an escape, and other than checking my empty email yesterday, I didn't let myself think of anything but him. He didn't give me time. We'd gone to the movies and I'd had another acupuncture appointment and we'd even worked out together.

"I guess it's time to get this over with," Liam says, walking into the room, and he is dark good looks personified, absolutely stunning in a light gray suit, his shirt starched and white, perfect, like he is to me. My eyes gravitate to the matching gray silk tie and I feel my body heat.

He closes the distance between us and pulls me to my feet. "You want me to tie you up again."

It's not a question. Embarrassed, I look down. His finger slides under my chin, lifting my gaze to his. "Don't be shy. It's just you and me, baby. Nothing we do goes beyond us. Nothing you tell me goes beyond me."

I wish that were true, but the more I know him, the more I know he will go after whoever is after me. And they will go after him. "Yesterday you were…different when we, ah…"

"Yesterday you didn't need me to force you to let go. You were already relaxed. Today, you're on edge. Why?"

I shut my eyes a moment. "I don't know."

"You don't want to be alone."

"I'm good at being alone, Liam."

"I don't want you to be good at being alone. You aren't alone anymore."

"It's too early for you to make promises like that."

"No. It's not. This thing between us isn't going away, but I've had more time in life to figure that out and you're afraid to count on me and us. We'll get by those things."

"You're so confident."

"About what I feel for you, yes."

"About everything."

"Not everything," he assures me. "You have this deer-in-headlights look sometimes that I'm sure means you're going to run. Run to me, Amy, not from me."

I wish I could promise him I would. Instead, I glower. "You are going to be late."

He doesn't budge, and the look on his face tells me he notices how I've avoided a promise I might not be able to keep. "Come with me to my meetings. There's a restaurant and shopping strip nearby you can hang out at, or I'll get you an office to work in."

My heart squeezes at his protectiveness. "I have a doctor's appointment you insisted on, and yes, I have work I've neglected that I'll end up not doing. Stop worrying about me. Your new design has you talking about this project all the time. You're passionate about it now. Go make it happen. Then you can stay here with me for a while."

"I keep telling you. I'm not going anywhere."

"Yes, you are. To your meeting so I can make my doctor's appointment."

"I'll drive you."

"It's two blocks. I'll walk. Go to your meetings, Liam."

"I'll be back as soon as possible." He runs his hand down the lavender silk blouse that matches my new lavender shorts, and I feel his touch in every part of me. I do not want him to go.

"Just seal the deal." I kiss him.

His hand goes to the back of my head and he slants his mouth over mine, deepening the kiss and leaving me breathless. "I plan to, baby," he assures me and sets me free, grabbing his briefcase and heading to the door. And I know he's not talking about the building. He's talking about me and him, and that sets me in action. I need a plan. A way out of this mess once and for all. No more waiting on someone else to make it go away. That hasn't worked.

Today I have a mission. Answers.

Chapter Seventeen

I've barely stepped out of the doctor's office when Liam sends me a text. How did the doctor go?

As well as any appointment that requires you stick your legs in stirrups.

And? He replies.

And yes, I got a sample package of pills. It is 7 days before I'm protected.

I can have a lot of fantasies in 7 days. What are you doing now?

Headed to walk by those properties and then do some research at the library.

What research?

Don't you have a meeting?

Yes dear, he jokes. I have a meeting. I'm actually being called back in now. I'll be tied up for a few hours but call me if you need me. I'll answer.

He'll answer, I type.

I stick my phone back in my purse and head for the bank. My stop is disappointing. There has been no further deposit and I worry now, though it hadn't crossed my mind while Liam and I were together, that I might have missed a message at the apartment. I find the door free of any plain white envelopes and consider knocking on Jared's door, but decide the mailbox is a better option. A private note would not be left in a public place. Not one that I wouldn't find before anyone else. I don't think I was given a key to the mailbox. I'll have to stop by to get one from Meg.

I'm about to turn back to the elevator when my door opens and a big, burly man exits. I scream and I am pretty sure my heart ceases to beat for a good sixty seconds. The door behind me opens and I whirl around and run straight at Jared, who grabs my arms.

"Whoa. Sweetheart. Easy. What's wrong?"

I blink up at Jared and my hands are all over his t-shirt that covers his rock-hard chest when they should not be, but he is the closest thing to safe I have right now. I turn in his arms and glare at the man in the front of my door, who has on some sort of overalls and sports a beer belly and some tools, and isn't quite as scary as he was a moment ago. "Why are you in my apartment?"

"Ms. Bensen?" he asks.

"Yes. Who are you?"

He chuckles. "You know people don't normally get excited to see me, but I don't usually send them running into another man's arms either. But hey, maybe that explains why I'm not dating. I'm scarier than I thought." He holds up a key. "I changed the locks like you ordered."

I let out a breath, and silently vow to make Liam pay for not warning me. "Yes. Sorry. I didn't know you were coming today." And how did Liam do this without a key but I quickly forget the question when I become aware of Jared's hand on my hip, his leg aligned with the back of mine. I step forward, out of his reach, and accept the key from the locksmith, who goes on to share some sort of mumbo-jumbo I do not hear.

Finally, he hands me the keys. "A maintenance guy came by and said they had to have a copy of the key as the management company. I didn't give it to him. Didn't know him from Adam. He wasn't pleased." He hands me papers and I sign.

"Thank you," I say and I mean it. "I'll get keys to them." Hopefully never, I mentally add. I don't care if I ever go back inside that apartment, but if Liam leaves, I'll have to.

THE SECRET LIFE OF AMY BENSON

Finally, the locksmith is gone and I turn to Jared, who looks way too amused. "Stop laughing at me," I order. "A single woman does not take a strange man coming out of her apartment lightly. That is foolish."

"I'm not complaining. It gave me a chance to get to know you better. Of course, you almost ran me over in the process. Didn't you know he was coming?"

"No. Yes. I did, but it slipped my mind. I've been busy."

"With the big, arrogant guy from the other day. Is he gone now?"

I grimace. "He's not arrogant. And no, he's not gone."

"But he's not here now."

"No. He's not here now."

He motions to his briefcase. "I'm headed to a place around the corner to drink a beer and get some work done. Want to join me?"

"Oh, ah, no. Thanks. I have some work of my own to do. I just came by to grab a file."

He stares at me, his brown eyes probing a bit too deeply, and I think maybe Liam is right. Maybe Jared is interested. I am so not equipped to handle two men of their caliber in the same day. "You want me to walk you down?"

"Down?"

"To the street."

"Yes. Sorry. The key guy rattled me. No. Go on without me. Thanks for, well, keeping me from doing who knows what."

His eyes dance with mischief, and a definite glint of warm brown heat. "At your service anytime."

He turns and saunters toward the elevator, all loose-legged confidence in jeans, that bad-boy sexiness oozing off of him. I'm not sure why I think the "bad boy" label fits him. It's a feeling, like the familiar one I normally have with him but I don't today, and that bothers me almost as much as when I do. I'm also not sure why I'm still staring after him when he stops at elevator and turns to catch me watching him. He grins at me and disappears inside the car.

***

I walk to the properties on my list I'm to visually inspect and report on, and they all seem occupied and well maintained. Everything seems as it should be, but my gut says it is not. At the final house on the list I find an elderly lady sitting in a rocking chair on her porch, and I approach her.

"Hi," I say. "I'm the property owner's assistant and he just wanted me to make sure everything is fine with the property."

"Howard!" the woman calls.

An elderly man appears at the door. "What, Bella?" He smiles at me. "Well hello, young lady."

"Did you hire a management company or something?" Bella asks.

He frowns. "No. Why would I do that? Been owning this place for ten years and done just fine by myself."

My heart sinks. "I'm sorry. I must have the wrong address. I'll correct my records."

It's official in my book. Everything is not as it should be. I walk away and make a beeline to the realtor's office, or rather, the law office, and even that is weird. It really is past due I find answers. My steps quicken and it hits me that there is a positive note to today. I don't have that "being followed" sensation. Answers, however do not seem to be in my immediate future. When I arrive at the Evernight office location, I find a sign that says "out to lunch." I glance at the time on my phone. How has it gotten to be 3:00? And how is 3:00 lunchtime?

I dial Meg again and leave a message and exchange another text with Liam before I decide I'm heading to the library. In the time I worked at the Central Branch in New York, I'd never used its resources beyond looking through some books. I'd been paranoid about bringing attention to myself. But then I took the job at the museum. I think I'm an extremist. I sure have been with my willingness to let Liam in my life and no one else.

I start walking toward a library I spotted a few blocks away when Meg calls back. "Sorry I missed you. Luke being out of

THE SECRET LIFE OF AMY BENSON

town is killing me. I have to keep running out to deal with tenants."

I prepare to turn around and go back to Evernight. "Are you heading back to the office?"

"I have another customer to deal with. You want to do happy hour? There's a restaurant/bar joint called Earl's right around the corner from your apartment. One of our customers took me there once. Looks like a great happy-hour spot."

I'll do whatever I have to in order to find the answers I need. "I'll find it. What time?"

"5:30?"

"I'll see you then."

We end the call and I continue on to the library, still remarkably without the sensation of being followed. I'm not sure if that means I'm without prying eyes or if I'm calmer now, and not conjuring demons where they might not be. Am I calmer now?

Once I'm at the library, I sit down at a long wooden table and consider where to dig into research, and as always when I'm thinking about the past, my mind radiates toward the tattoo on my handler's wrist. If I find a link to him, I find a link to whatever, or whomever, I'm running from. I consider what I've already considered in the past. I've always been certain the triangle shape relates to the pyramids, since my father had done much of his work in Egypt, but I have nothing that makes the exact image of the tattoo connect to anything that confirms this.

I shut my eyes and picture Liam's tattoo. The numbers beneath it form a triangle. I don't like where my mind is going, and I pull my computer out of the small leather briefcase Liam bought me while shopping and Google the "pi" sign. Nowhere is there a similar image with numbers forming an inverted triangle. And the symbol on my handler's arm was a triangle with words inside, words that I'd thought to be another language, but had since decided was some sort of coded message. It isn't like Liam's tattoo at all. Not even close. My stomach knots. Except for the triangle. I draw in a heavy breath. Liam's interest in pyramids is a

169

coincidence that's hard to ignore. But lots of people are intrigued by pyramids, I remind myself he's an architect, looking for an answer as to how they were created. Perhaps solving the mystery is a personal challenge. It's a logical interest, especially for someone who mastered his craft at such a young age.

I key "mathematical symbols" into my search bar and scan image after image in search of the symbol I'm looking for. I find triangles but nothing that is a real match. Same story I always end up with. Finally, I force myself to stop putting off what I really came here for. Today I will do what I haven't had the courage to do ever. I walk to one of the tables with archived material and search for old newspaper clippings of the night my life changed forever. Or I try. There is not one single reference to a fire in my hometown the year or month when it occurred. Nothing. That is just...odd.

Back at the table, I Google my father and start listing every name ever associated with him I can find. I'm surprised at how few links I find on him, considering he was responsible for carving out more than a few pieces of history. My heart squeezes when I think of being with him when one of his great discoveries had been made. I shove aside the bittersweet memory and refocus on research. What would make someone want to kill him, and everyone he loved? What would make them hunt me down?

Maybe it's not about his archeological finds. He sat on government committees and became involved in international relations, and not long before he died there was talk of his retirement from field work and a political appointment in Washington. I shake my head. I don't know where this is taking me. I was young, and uninvolved in that part of his life. I know nothing about it. If I'm still a target, and I am, then someone thinks I know something I shouldn't. It's only logical. They can't hurt my father by killing me. He's already dead.

I decide to make a list of everyone I ever knew or knew my family to know, here and overseas, when my brother and I would go on digs with my father. Next, I cross-reference it with the Google searches. I stare at the list. It's sixty names long and I don't even know what I'm looking for. My first instinct is to mark everyone off that has nothing to do with my father, but I change my mind. I've hyper-focused on this being about him and his work.

It's not about the money. It was never about the money. My mother's voice flashes through my mind. My mind was trying to tell me something, but what? Who was she talking to? Who was there that day?

***

Remarkably, I do not have a flashback while doing my research, and I wonder if that has something to do with feeling like I'm taking control and finding answers. At 5:00 I force myself to pack up and head to my meeting with Meg. Finding Earl's Restaurant and Bar is easier than I expect, and I arrive at 5:15. A waitress points me to the left and I enter a bar area with huge booths that sit on pedestals above rows of tables, and directly opposite the huge wooden bar. I choose the booth at the very back where I can see Meg when she enters, and I have plenty of room to put my computer to use while I wait.

I've barely settled into my seat when a waitress appears to take my order of a house red wine. I open my computer and look directly in front of me and go still. Jared is sitting at the next booth over, facing me, his computer open and a beer by his side.

I swallow the dryness in my throat and he motions to my table, asking to join me. I nod, unsure why this makes me guilty. He's a neighbor, not my new lover, but I know Liam wouldn't approve—and honestly, if I found him having drinks with some hot woman, I wouldn't either.

He slides into the half-moon-shaped booth, and to my relief, remains directly across from me. "Past due we get some quality time together," he says, as the waitress sets my wine down beside me.

"I wasn't aware we were trying to get quality time together."

"Well, now you are," he says with a smile, and there is this casual sexy thing about him that screams completely relaxed and comfortable in his own skin. And I'm sure many women would

171

be comfortable in it too. But not me. I prefer the edgy, dark thing Liam wears like a second skin.

"You really are a smartass, aren't you?" I ask, but it's really not a question. He is.

"Most of the time."

"Why?"

"Comes natural, like being arrogant does for your boyfriend."

Boyfriend? Is that what Liam is to me? And somehow, it seems too small a word for him. "I'd defend him, but I don't think it would do me any good."

"Good call." Amusement fills his dark eyes and he is absolutely Mr. Bad Boy Sexy in this moment. "What are you working on?"

"Just playing around while I wait for a friend to join me." There. Avoidance. I'm still good at it with everyone but Liam. "What about you?"

"I'm doing high-tech work on contract."

"High-tech work? You don't seem like a computer geek."

"What do I seem like?"

"The long hair and ripped jeans and...well, something more...rowdy."

He laughs. "Rowdy. I'm not sure how to take that, but basically I'm a professional hacker. I'm hired to try to hack a site, and if I can, they then pay me to make sure no one else can. I do a lot of defense contractor work."

Bad-boy hacker. That fits him. "Thus the Boeing shirt?"

"Thus the Boeing shirt. Normally I'm holed up in a hotel for a month or so on a job, but a friend was laid off and had to relocate for a job, which stuck him with the apartment. At six grand a month in rent, he was eager to have someone supplement the cost."

"Six grand? How big is your place? I only pay two."

He laughs. "You must have a fan somewhere. There isn't an apartment in the building under six grand. We're in prime real estate and in the center of a high-profile restaurant and shopping area."

"Oh, well, I think my boss owns the building."

"Who's your boss?"

I hesitate, not sure why. "Dermit Williams."

"Never heard of him. I thought a big holding company owned the building."

"Hello!" Meg appears by the table, looking every bit the blonde bombshell I can never be in a snug black dress and I'm rattled to realize I hadn't even noticed her approach. She hugs me and then glances at Jared. "Good grief, woman, you hang out with beautiful people. I'm sitting with him." She scoots Jared over, and next to me. I'm ready to crawl under the table.

"Please," Jared says approvingly. "Come on in." He glances down at me. "Hope you don't mind getting up close and personal."

Somehow I am captured in his warm brown stare, and I feel the connection in the pit of my stomach, more in the form of guilt than attraction. Not that I am beyond seeing how hot this man is. He is, and if I were any other woman, I suspect I'd be glad to be here, but I'm not. I'm a woman who is crazy about another man, and the fact that Jared makes me think of Liam speaks of just how intensely drawn to Liam I am. My cell phone beeps with a text and Meg and Jared chat with the waitress while I pull out my phone.

Where are you?

Earl's. I met Meg for a drink.

I wait for a reply but don't get one. Odd. I shut my computer and stick it back in my briefcase, preparing for a fast departure if I get any more uncomfortable.

"I will be soooo happy when Luke gets back," Meg announces, and I grab the opening she gives me.

"Did you ask him for that number I needed from him?"

The waitress delivers her wine and she thanks her before saying, "Yes. And sorry. He won't give it out." She turns to Jared. "I haven't been introduced."

"Jared," he says. "And you are?"

"Meg." She offers her hand and he turns to her and accepts it. She bats her lashes in a flirtatious way I've spent too much time staying off the radar to ever even attempt. I can't see Jared's expression the way he's positioned, but I can't imagine there is a man on the planet who wouldn't pant over Meg's ample beauty. They both settle into their seats again and Meg asks, "And what do you do for a living, Jared? Where are you from? Are you single?"

I just about choke on a swallow of wine. Jared laughs. "Tech guy. Texas. And yes"—he glances at me—"I'm single."

I officially have cotton in my throat. I grab my wine and take a big swig. Jared laughs, clearly amused at my reaction, proof my decision to stay away from men while living off the radar had been a good idea. They send my composure into the dumpster. Or, at least, men like Jared and Liam, who are exceptionally…male.

"And how do you know Amy?" Meg queries Jared.

"I'm renting the apartment across from her."

I tilt my head and frown, thinking of my extreme rent difference to what Jared has stated. "He's staying in a friend's apartment. That's probably why you don't know him."

"Why would she know me?" Jared asks.

"She works in the management office," I supply.

"New, though." She seems almost uneasy, but then being new is never fun and she adds, "I'm just learning the ropes and learning who is where and what is what." She sips her wine. "This isn't what I ordered. I'm going to the bar. Be right back."

Great. Alone with Jared again. And why hasn't Liam texted me back? "Where are you from, Amy?" Jared asks.

On a conflicting note, I've been craving a chance to talk to him about my hometown and avoided it at the same time. Apparently, I'm going to talk to him about Texas. "New York. You're from Texas, you said?"

"Yes. Ever been there?"

"No. Too many pickup trucks and football fans." Lie. That is a part of Texas that makes it Texas, and I miss it.

"And beer." He lifts his bottle and takes a drink. "Us Texans like our beer."

Not this one. "You can keep it. I don't like it."

"Ever tried this one?" He shows me the bottle with some sort of special import label.

"Never."

"Try it." He offers me his bottle. "It's a different taste altogether."

He wants me to drink from his bottle? "No. No thank you."

Meg returns. "Ohhh, I'd love to try it."

He hands her the bottle and she takes a sip. "German?"

"Yes. German."

"Try it, Amy," Meg encourages. "German beers are completely different from the American version."

Jared hands me the bottle, a challenge in his eyes. Somehow, I feel as if me drinking from his bottle is some sort of ploy to tear down a wall he thinks will let him get closer to me, but I feel like a deer in headlights, with both him and Meg watching me.

I grab the bottle and take a drink, the bitter taste filling my mouth, and I grimace a moment before awareness prickles down my spine. I glance up to find Liam striding toward us, and he is not only the picture of male perfection in his gray suit, his dark hair neatly groomed, his goatee finely trimmed, his jaw is set solid, his eyes hard. He's pissed. He saw me drinking from Jared's bottle.

He stops beside me and takes my hand. "Let's go, Amy."

I'm appalled. Did he really just order me to leave? "Liam—"

He lowers his head and presses his mouth to my ear. "Let's go now."

My emotions are a rollercoaster ride of anger, embarrassment, and more anger. I slip my briefcase and purse on over my shoulder and scoot out of my seat, and I don't look directly at Jared or Meg. "I forgot we had a dinner meeting tonight."

"Amy—" Jared starts.

"Don't," Liam says sharply.

I pull away from him and start walking for the door. He's behind me. I don't have to look to know. I feel the predator in him. Well, he's going to find out that this deer in headlights just grew fangs.

Chapter Eighteen

I exit the restaurant and I don't stop walking. I'm going to the apartment I swore I wouldn't go back to anytime soon, not his hotel. I've spent too much time feeling like I don't own me, and now he wants to own me. No. No, this is not going to happen. I've been "insane" over this man. Clearly insane.

I'm crossing the street when Liam shackles my wrist, claiming control and all but dragging me with him, the big bully. "Let go, Liam."

"Not a chance. Not until we're in the room."

"I'm not going to the room with you."

He doesn't even look at me. "Like hell you're not."

"I'll make a scene."

He stops at the curb on the other side of the road, and turns to me, his eyes hard, his voice crackling with barely contained anger. "No. You won't." It's a command he expects me to follow, solidified by the way he starts walking again, tugging me along with him.

"Liam—"

"Don't talk, Amy. You'll only piss me off more."

He's pissed off? I'm the one who has been embarrassed and treated like crap. I'm the one who is angry. He won't intimidate me. He won't control me like this. He wants to go at it with me, I'm in. Bring it on.

We reach the hotel in record speed. The doorman says hello to us and Liam doesn't even look at him, and I'm pretty sure we're a walking billboard for a couple about to go to war. Oh, yes. We are getting good at making scenes and getting noticed. I'm failing miserably at staying off the radar, and I have Liam to thank for that. No, I amend again. I have me to thank for that. I let this happen. I let him happen, and I have to do something about it.

We enter the elevator and he slides his card through the panel and then pulls me hard against him, forcing my hands to his chest, with nowhere else to go. My legs settle against his, and damn it, I am affected, wet and aching for him, and this only serves to spike my anger a notch higher. He's controlling me and I don't like it. I can feel him willing me to look at him and I refuse.

As if punishing me for my insubordination, his hand slides down my back and cups my backside, caressing deeply, and I swear I feel it like a stroke between my thighs. Barely containing a moan, I curl my fingers around his shirt and I want to scream with the injustice of how aroused I am.

The doors to the elevator slide open and my heart jackhammers. The adrenaline pouring through me is like acid in my blood, burning me with anticipation. The swipe of his card on his door feels eternal, almost slow motion, and then Liam is dragging me inside the hallway and I am against the wall.

"Stop shoving me around, Liam. Stop trapping me, and—"

His mouth comes down hard on mine, a deep thrust of his tongue claiming me, the taste of his anger like a shot of spicy, bitter whiskey about to pull me into a haze I cannot allow myself to enter. I shove at his chest and he tears his mouth from mine, and I am both relieved and tormented by the loss of the intimate connection.

"You have no right to do what you did back there," I hiss.

"You made that pretty damn clear tonight."

"I didn't do anything, Liam. You did."

"What I did was have a shit day you completed with an exclamation mark." He shrugs out of his jacket and tosses it aside, then does the same with his tie.

"I repeat. I didn't do this. You did."

He leans on the wall. "And you know how I wanted to deal with this shit day? I wanted to get lost in you, and us, and what did I find? You with him."

"He was there when I got there."

"And that made you drink out of his bottle." It's not a question. It's an accusation. His hand slides into my hair, and he stares down at me, his hand moving roughly over my shirt. "I have no right, you say? That's what it comes down to, now doesn't it? I have no right to want you all to myself. I have no right to expect you to be loyal."

"You—"

He rips my shirt and I gasp as he unsnaps my bra, teasing my nipple, pinching it. He is rough, hard in a way I've never known him to be. "I liked this shirt and now it's ruined," I whisper, but I'm not talking about the shirt. I'm talking about us.

"And you like being fucked. So that's what I'm going to do. Maybe you want me to be that guy I was before I met you. Maybe you want me to fuck you and leave you. Or maybe you'd rather him do it."

"No." My voice is barely audible. I feel defeated. He unbuttons my shorts and I let him. "I don't want Jared."

He shoves my shorts and panties down my hips and his fingers are between my thighs, stroking the sensitive flesh before the clothes ever hit the floor. "Maybe," he adds, acid in his tone, "we should invite Meg and Jared over to join us."

Hurt and anger overcome me. "Is that what you want? Permission to go back to what you were before me? To fuck everyone and anyone?"

"You're nice and wet just talking about it—"

"Stop!" I shove at his chest. "Stop talking like that and stop touching me."

He surprises me and lets me go, leaving me standing there with my shirt ripped open and my shorts at my feet. He motions to the door. "You want me to stop. You want to go. Then go."

I hug myself. "Who are you? I don't even know you."

"I can only be me, baby, and I'm not sure you can say the same. I'm not sure you know who you are and I damn sure don't."

The insult that hits a little too close to home, like a slap, and I slump. "If you wanted to hurt me, it worked." I kick off the shorts and throw them at him. "Keep your stupid clothes and money and asshole attitude." I cut around him, not even caring I'm in a ripped shirt and sandals and nothing else, and I don't stop until I'm at the dresser digging for my clothes that I bought. I've been alone a long time. I can do it again. I will do it again.

Liam's hand comes down on my arm and he turns me. "What are you doing?"

"Putting on my clothes that don't make me feel like some kind of prostitute you own."

"Prostitute. How can you even say that? You were the one with someone else."

"I wasn't with him, Liam. I was with you. Was as in past."

He pulls me to him and the heat of his body, the feel of him pressed to me, is heaven and hell at the same time. I want him. I need him. But not like this. Not. Like. This. "Is that what you want?" he demands. "Me gone? Me out of your life?"

I know I should say "yes." I should walk away and get out of what is trouble waiting to happen. "You're being an ass."

"Do you want me out of your life, Amy?"

"No," I whisper. "I don't want you out of my life. I want you to stop acting like this."

His mouth comes down on mine and it is hot and possessive and it is not heaven and hell this time. It is heaven, and I sink into the kiss, melt into his body, the argument and the rest of the world disappearing. I am connected to this man. I need him like I didn't think I could need.

I grab his shirt and I pay him back for what he did to mine. I rip it open, letting buttons fly, and my hands push under the cloth, absorbing warm skin and taut muscle. I wrap myself around him. I cannot get close enough to him.

He lifts me onto the dresser against the wall and I do not even remember him shoving his pants down. There is just his mouth on mine, his hands on my breast, and the hard length of him pressing between my thighs, into the wet, sensitive V of my body.

He is as he has never been with me. I am as I have never been with anyone. Wild, out of control. He is kissing me everywhere, whiskers rasping erotically over my skin, tongue licking and tasting, and driving me insane. His hands curve under my backside, arching me against him, and he pumps into me, drives harder and harder until we are so lost in passion, we cling to each other, our heads buried in each other's necks, our bodies moving fiercely, urgently.

The edge of release comes over me in an unexpected, intense rush—too fast, and not fast enough. I gasp with the clenching of my muscles and then I am there, tumbling into the dark place that is not danger but pleasure, millions of sensations rolling through me, overwhelming me. In some distant part of my mind, I register Liam's groan, the shake of his body, the tension in his muscles. For long moments, or perhaps minutes, we just hold each other. Time stands still and then slowly comes back to me. It is then that I become aware of the dampness between my thighs and the reality of what has just happened. Panic rises in me. Flashes of fire burn in my mind.

"Get off me," I order. "Get off. Let me down from the dresser." My heart is thundering and my hands are shaking.

Liam leans back, looking baffled. "Amy—"

"Let me go, Liam. Let me go now."

There is a stunned look on his face, but he doesn't argue. He pulls out of me and he tries to help me off the dresser, but I don't let him. I jump off the edge and run to the bathroom, grabbing a towel and cleaning myself up. I can feel him behind me, watching me. I can't even clean up without him hovering. I can't control my life when he's controlling it, and yet another eruption of emotion is on me before I can stop it.

I whirl on him. "We didn't use a condom."

He runs a hand through his hair. "The chances that—"

"Don't downplay it. Don't tell me the odds of me being pregnant are slim." My voice cracks. I think I might cry. "There is a chance. There's a big chance." I look down and I'm still in my stupid sandals, though somehow my shirt is gone. I look ridiculous and I don't care. "I cannot be pregnant. I can't be."

"Is having my baby that horrible?"

"My God. You of all people who have women chasing your money should be freaked out right now."

"I'm not."

"You should be. You should be, Liam. I don't know why you don't get it. Everyone in my life dies. They die. Our baby—" He steps toward me and I hold up a hand. "Don't even think about it. You acted like an ass tonight and this is what happened. This is where it got us."

"I'll protect you. I won't let anything happen to you."

"Do you think my father wanted to let my mother die?" I'm shouting. I never shout but I'm shouting. "You can't protect me. No one can." I've said too much, but it's too late. I can't even seem to care. My chest is heaving, my body trembling.

He stares at me, and the torment in his eyes rips through my emotions and creates more. I am on overload, tunneling into the abyss, and I do not know what to do. Suddenly, I feel him, rather than my panic. He's hurt. He's really hurt. I don't want to care, but I do. "Liam—"

He turns and disappears. I stare after him and fight through a million emotions. He was an ass tonight and I should be furious, but there was something in him just now, really during this whole encounter, that I have never felt from him. Something painful.

I grab the red silk robe he'd given me from the back of the door and tie it around me before seeking Liam out. I find him on the couch, his elbows on his knees, his head on his hands. "Liam?"

He looks up at me and there is more turbulence, more darkness. "You're right. I was an ass. My father called today, and it's not an excuse. It's just a fact. I always say I won't let him mess with my head, but he does."

"Your father? I thought he was gone?"

"Like I said. Sharks swimming at my feet, baby. He only calls when he wants money or he's in trouble. It started out with him wanting to make amends, and have his son back in his life years ago, but it was only about money."

Oh, God. The way he values honesty makes sense now. I want to go to him but I'm afraid he'll stop talking. "He just…" He scrubs his jaw and starts again. "He was drunk driving today and hit a car with a family in it."

I grab my stomach. "Oh, God. No."

He nods. "A little girl's mother is now in intensive care and she was in the car while her mother almost bled to death. I'd just found out when I went to Earl's. I felt like being with you would somehow…" He hesitates. "I saw you with him, and I snapped. I'm sorry."

I rush forward and I go down on my knees in front of him, my hands settling on his knee. "I'm sorry. I would never make you feel like I made you feel tonight on purpose."

"You didn't make me feel this. I did. I think maybe I have a little too much of my pops in me for both our good."

"No. You were human tonight, Liam."

"You don't get it. Every time he does this, I crawl out of my own skin. I have to go to New York. I booked the last flight out tonight."

I don't even hesitate in my response. "I'll go with you." He needs me. I have to be there for him. I won't be anywhere anyone will find me. I'll be with Liam. I'll be safe.

"No. This will hit the papers and if you're with me, you will, too. We both know you can't have that happen."

I'm taken aback. What does he mean? What does he know? "Liam—"

"We've already established you don't want to be around me when I'm like this. I'm not done being an ass. I've got a lot more of my father to deal with and a lot more of the me you don't like to follow."

"I can deal with you being an ass now that I know why."

"I can't. Just please stay here in the hotel where I know you're safe. There are cameras and security, especially in this suite. I need to know you're safe."

He's decided. I hear it in his voice. "Yes. Okay. I'll stay, but I really want to go with you."

"Stay, Amy. And think about tonight when I'm gone."

"There's nothing to think about."

"We both know that's not true." He sets me aside and pushes to his feet.

I follow him to the bedroom and sit on the bed while he changes into faded jeans and a light blue pullover, and boots, then fills a suitcase. "When will you be back?"

"I don't know. I have to take care of this kid my father hurt and her family, and get him back into rehab."

Back into rehab. This is very much an ongoing battle for Liam.

"Where's your phone?" he asks.

"I don't know. I don't even remember dropping my purse or briefcase when we came in the door."

His jaw tenses and he turns away, returning with my things. "I want you to put Derek's number in your phone. I know you don't know him, but he's like a brother to me. I trust him and so can you."

I pull out my phone and Liam takes it, keying in the number for me before going down on a knee in front of me. His expression softens and his fingers caress down my cheek. "For the record, we'd make beautiful babies together."

My breath lodges in my throat and I lean into him, resting my forehead on his. "I don't want you to go."

"I just hope you want me to come back." He kisses my forehead and then digs out the key to the car, pressing it to my palm. "I'll take a cab. Use it if you need it." He reaches behind him and pulls out his wallet and a credit card.

I shake my head. "No, Liam."

"I'm not getting on this plane thinking you might need something I can't give you. Take it. The pin is 1117. We will both have peace of mind in knowing you have it if you need it."

Reluctantly, I nod and accept it. "Hurry back."

He pushes to his feet, stares down at me for several seconds and then grabs his bag and starts walking. Fighting the urge to chase after him, I dig my fingers into the blanket and wait for the sound I dread. The door opening and shutting with him on the outside.

I am alone again.

Chapter Nineteen

$$\pi$$

I wake up the next morning in an empty bed, with my cell phone on the pillow where I wish Liam's head were resting. He didn't call. He'd sent me a text message when he landed in New York that was nothing more than Are you okay? followed by walking into the hospital when I'd confirmed I was fine. I'd called him several times but he had not answered.

Sitting up, I scan the room that has oddly begun to feel like home, but today it is an empty shell and I have nothing to fill it with. It scares me how wrong I feel without Liam. How quickly I have become used to waking up to him. My phone beeps with a text and I quickly click on it.

This is why I didn't want you here. There is a link and I click on it. The headline reads, Billionaire's father arrested on DUI. The subtitle though is the worst part. Mother of two almost bleeds to death while young daughter watches. I read the details of what has been reported and my gut knots at the horrific article that all but calls it Liam's fault for not controlling his father. I dial his number. He doesn't answer. I text him. Please call me.

Walking into courthouse is the reply I receive.

He doesn't want to talk to me. I feel it. He needed me last night and he feels like I wasn't there for him. Maybe I have a little too much of my pops in me for both our good. My confident, talented man isn't as confident as I thought. Somehow the vulnerability in him makes him more human, more special. But he doesn't think so. He thinks of himself as damaged goods.

My hand settles on my belly and I hate the certainty that if I am pregnant I'll have to leave Liam. He is too high profile, too newsworthy, and my child and I would therefore be in the spotlight, where we would become bigger targets than I already am. I see why Alex hated the press. Liam is media fodder whether he wants to be or not. I don't want to leave him. I don't want to run anymore. That means I cannot sit back and hope I am not found. I can't go on trying to find answers in a scared and non-committed way.

Decision made to act and quickly, I throw off the blanket, rush through a shower, and then dress in jeans, a tank top, and Keds. I leave the hotel on a mission for answers, and make my now daily stop by the bank, where I disappointedly find nothing has changed. There is not more money in my account. The discovery serves as reinforcement for what I have to do next. If Liam were to suddenly be out of my life, I have to be able to survive and not end up dead.

I swing by the cell phone store, where I buy several disposable phones. A few blocks later, I stop at Evernight to find another "out to lunch" sign. I call Meg and she actually answers. "Please tell me you're okay. I tried to call you this morning. I was worried after that man of yours acted like an oaf."

"I didn't see the call." In fact, I'm quite certain there wasn't one, so this lie bothers me. "I'm fine. Liam had a family emergency and he overreacted to Jared because of it."

"Oh no. I hope everything is okay?"

I think better of telling her he's out of town. "It's under control. I've been trying to connect with you on the properties I was given to inspect. I really don't think I have the right list. If I email you the list, can you confirm if I do or don't?"

"Sure. Of course." She gives me her direct email address. "You want to try happy hour again?"

No. "I'm tied up for the next few days. Maybe mid-week. I'll email you the list today."

"Yes. Okay." She sounds awkward, but who wouldn't after what she witnessed last night? "You might want to call Jared. He was worried about you."

"I don't even have his number."

"I'll text it to you."

"Thanks." No thanks is more like it.

We end the call and she indeed sends me Jared's number by text, which I delete. I have no intention of letting Jared know my cell number, and hopefully Meg won't give it to him. As it is, the mystery blocked-number call has me uneasy.

I grab a few groceries that will allow me to keep my slim budget in check and hole up in the hotel room for a few days, intending to do nothing but research. I set up a workstation on the dining room table and then dial Liam. He doesn't answer. I text him. No reply. I try not to think the worst, like he's shutting me out intentionally, or that I'm still here in his rented room, out of some obligation he feels to protect me. It's not hard to believe that could be true, with the news piece blaming him for his father's sins. Guilt, no matter how unwarranted, has to be his enemy right now.

Settling into a chair at the dining room table, I prepare a notepad and have my computer on and ready. My first priority is to send Meg the property listings, then I break out the disposable phones. I begin making calls, pretending to be a reporter from a New York paper who is doing a story on my father's life and death. No one can find records of the fire. This is illogical. There was a fire. I'm not crazy. I didn't imagine that life-changing event.

Hours pass and I make call after call to museums, media outlets, records departments, and old connections I know are linked to my father. It seems I blink and the room is dim, the sunlight gone. I flip on lights and check my inbox and find nothing from Meg on the property listing I sent her. I call her and she replies by text. Working late. Will call you tomorrow.

A knock sounds on the door and I stand up, staring in the direction of the entryway. No one knows I'm here. Liam has stopped evening housekeeping visits. I'm not being paranoid. I'm being realistic. This could be a problem. More knocking sounds. I decide I'm going to pretend I'm not here. My cell phone starts ringing and I glance down to find the caller ID reads "Derek". I am relieved. Someone will be on the phone with me if this door knocking turns into a problem.

"Hello," I answer.

"Amy, this is Derek. Do you know who I am?"

"Liam's friend."

"Liam's friend who is standing at your door with a delivery from him."

"Oh. Sorry. I was—"

"Being smart like any woman alone should be, but let me in, will ya?"

"Yes. On my way." I end the call and rush toward the door.

Opening it up, I find a tall, good-looking blond man about Liam's age, in a well-tailored navy suit, holding plastic grocery bags. He lifts them slightly. "I bring food."

What? "Am I on Candid Camera?"

He chuckles. "If you are, we both are, and I think I might be the one getting laughed at." He enters the hall and keeps walking, leading me to the mini-fridge in the main room of the suite. He deposits the bags on the counter. "Liam didn't trust you to spend your money, or his, on groceries. He didn't want you to go hungry." He starts putting away the groceries.

"I can't believe he asked you to do this. I can't believe you really did it."

"He's worried about you."

"He can't keep spending money on me."

He glances over his shoulder. "You do know he's a billionaire, right?"

"Sometimes I wish he wasn't."

He shuts the fridge and leans on the counter, crossing his arms over his chest. "I have to hear this. Do explain."

Liam's words about his father, about many people, I suspect, come back to me. Sharks swimming at my feet. "How will he ever know I want him and not his money?"

189

His expression softens. "He knows, Amy. Believe me, he knows, or you wouldn't be here and neither would I."

"He won't even take my calls."

"He's messed up right now."

"Over his father."

"Yes. Over his father. Give him a little time."

I don't like how that sounds. "How long do you think he'll be gone?"

"A few days. We have to finalize him as the architect on this project by next week or he's out. He seems to want in."

"If he gets to use his design."

"You seem to know him pretty well for someone who just came into his life. That's good. He's been alone a long time."

Liam has been alone a long time. I'm still thinking about that a few minutes later when I shut the door behind Derek, promising to lock up and call him if I need anything. I like Derek and decide I will call him if I need to. I just hope I don't need to. I dial Liam. He doesn't answer. No surprise there. I shower and pull on one of his shirts and call again. Still he doesn't answer.

***

Two days pass, and Liam has only texted me a few times. I'm going crazy and it's Sunday, so I'm limited on distractions. I can't make much progress on the phone and the library in walking distance is closed. Monday comes with a text from Liam checking on me that leaves me feeling more alone than ever. I dress and arrive at the library when it opens, and my hunt through their microfilm collection takes up most of the day.

Tuesday arrives with another text and drives me into more research. While I am no closer to answers about my past, I actually connect with someone who can change my identity completely. The catch: it will cost me ten thousand dollars I don't have. The alternative is a flea-market fake that will at least allow me to travel inside the States. At fifty dollars, it wins me over and I decide getting one is on my Wednesday agenda as a safety precaution.

It's nearly nine o'clock when Derek stops by again. I greet him at the door, feeling rather hostile at his presence. "Why are you here to check up on me for him but he can't call me?"

"Amy—"

"Answer the question."

He scrubs his jaw. "He's dealing with his father's trash talk and it messes with his head more than you can possibly know."

"Exactly, because he's shut me out."

"He'll come around. Let me take you to dinner."

"No. I'm staying here. Thank you, though." I don't invite him in.

"Liam says you need a job."

"I have one."

He studies me a moment. "Then why does he think you don't?"

"I'll ask him if he calls me."

He sighs heavily. "Call me if you need me."

Guilt over my shortness is instant. "I'm sorry. Thank you. I will."

He leaves, and while I'm no longer hostile, I'm determined. The silence has to end. I call Liam and he doesn't answer. That's it. I'm taking action. I text him. Call me or I'm getting on a plane and finding you. And if you think I won't do it, you don't know me well.

My cell rings instantly. I answer to hear, "Amy." His voice is sandpaper rough, almost brittle.

"I guess your quick call means you really want to stop me from showing up there."

"I don't want you in this part of my life."

He thinks he's bad for me. I think I'm bad for him. "You aren't your father."

"You won't convince him of that." Bitterness and pain ripple through his words.

"Let me come there and be with you."

"No. You will end up in the newspapers."

"And you don't want me there."

191

"I don't."

I flinch. "Okay. I get it. I'm going to go back to my apartment—"

"No. Shit. Don't. Please. I'm handling this all wrong, just like I did the other night in Earl's. Look. Amy. I'm not the person I want you to know right now. That's why I haven't called. I don't know what will come out of my mouth, but thinking about being back there with you is all that keeps me sane."

My eyes pinch. "Just come back," I whisper. "When can you come back?"

"Soon."

"Promise. I know how you feel about promises."

"I promise." He hesitates. "Amy—"

"Yes?" I hold my breath and wait, not sure what to expect.

He lets out a breath. "Tell me you won't leave."

"I won't leave."

"Promise."

I squeeze my eyes shut. If I make this promise I have to tell him everything when he gets back. He can't protect himself from a danger he doesn't know exists. And I'm pretty certain he'd come after me if I left anyway. "I promise."

***

Wednesday morning I am at the bank when it opens to discover my account is as empty as my inbox remains. I'm frustrated with Meg's "out with a client" and "haven't had time to check the listings" text messages. Surely her boss has to have returned to town, and I head in that direction. When I find the office closed again, I do not feel good about this. I decide to walk to the back door and see if I can get into the building to look around.

Once I'm in the small alleyway, I knock on the door to be safe, and receive no response. I try the door but it's locked. There is a window that has to be Luke's office and I decide to try it, praying I don't get myself arrested. I peek in the window to find an empty office, without furniture or even boxes. The window is locked, so I move to the window on the opposite side of the building to find it's vacant. Unease ripples through me. Something is very wrong about this. There could be another office, but from the lobby it looked very small inside. I don't know what to do.

As much as I dread it, I know I need to stop by the apartment and look for any notes. I still have no mail key since I can't connect with Meg, but I'll check my door.

I arrive to find nothing on my door or under it. Hesitating, I turn to Jared's door and decide to knock. He doesn't answer. Figures.

Deciding it is Meg and Luke I need to be researching, I stop by INK coffee shop near the hotel to splurge on a mocha to take with me to the room. I've just ordered when I hear, "Amy."

I turn and find Jared sitting in a corner chair with his computer in his lap, his long, light brown hair loose around his shoulders, and that familiar feeling roars through me more powerfully than ever. He motions for me to join him and I hold up a finger, then grab my coffee and join him, claiming the empty seat next to him. "I've been worried about you," he insists. "After that guy dragged you from Earl's, I wasn't sure what to think."

"He'd had a family emergency and was worried about losing it in the bar."

His eyes narrow. "That's your story and you're sticking with it, right?"

"It's my story because it's true."

He closes his laptop and sets it aside, and my gaze catches on his University of Texas graduation ring. And I know now why Jared is familiar. I must have seen the ring, and my subconscious registered it when I did not. He has a connection to my brother and an image of Chad flashes in my mind. My fingers dig into my leg. I see his face. I actually see his face.

"You look like you saw a ghost," Jared comments, and I jerk my gaze to his.

"You went to UT?" I ask, and I sound strange, but I feel strange, too.

Jared glances at his ring. "I did. Why do you ask?"

193

"Way back when, I considered attending." Because I wanted to follow in my brother's footsteps and convince my father I was as good as Chad.

"Why didn't you?"

"New York was home so it made more sense." It's a lie I tell easily. I don't like this connection I have to Jared, but it seems he wouldn't wear the ring if he wanted to hide it.

"How long ago did you graduate?" I ask, trying to find out if he could be linked to my brother.

"I'm twenty-eight if that's what you want to know."

Chad would be thirty now. "I'm twenty-four."

"So, not long out of school," he observes.

"A few years."

"What did you study?"

"Nothing exciting. Business. How does someone get into hacking?"

"Generally by getting into trouble. I had a knack and did a few high-profile hack jobs just to prove I could. A narrow miss with the law and a close family friend shook me up." He sips his coffee and I do the same. "You don't seem to be staying at the apartment."

"You just keep missing me. I've been in and out early and late." I push to my feet. "I need to run. Good seeing you."

"Good seeing you too, Amy. Maybe I'll catch up to you again soon."

I step onto the street, and all I can think is what looks like a goldfish in the pond could be a shark swimming at my feet. Nothing is right and everything is wrong. I think I need to leave before I pull Liam into the quicksand that is swallowing me. But if I leave, I'm not sure he will look for me, even if it's only out of obligation, and he will put himself at risk. I don't know what to do. I need a plan, but my mind just keeps flashing an image of the graduation ring on Jared's hand, blocking out everything else. The connection between him and my brother seems too coincidental. They could have been in school together. But what about the empty offices at Evernight?

THE SECRET LIFE OF AMY BENSON

The pinching sensation in my forehead begins. I speed up and head for the hotel, certain I need to get out of public and fast. I manage to get to the hotel elevator when I see a flash of my brother's face. So clear. So perfect, when I've not been able to picture him for years. That's how powerfully Jared's ring has impacted me.

Leaning on the wall, I will away the image of my brother I'd otherwise welcome, praying I make it to the room without collapsing. My hand shakes as I swipe the key across the security panel and then shove open the door. I make a beeline to the safety of the bed and lie down. My cell phone rings but the spots are before my eyes and I see only darkness.

"Where's your mother?"

Lying on the bed on my belly, a book in front of me, I jump at the unexpected, unfamiliar harshness of my father's voice and find him in my doorway. "I don't know. She left a while ago."

"How long ago?"

"A few hours."

"Be more specific, Amy. You know I like details."

The sound of an engine and tires on gravel signals her arrival and he is already gone, stomping down the stairs. I rush to the window, parting the curtains to see him yank her out of the car and shove her against the door. I gasp and press my hand to my mouth. My father has never touched any of us. Their voices lift, loud enough to echo through the air, and be heard by neighbors, but I cannot understand the words no matter how hard I try.

I blink against black and white dots, and a wave of nausea overcomes me. Throwing away the blankets, I rush to the bathroom and go down on my knees in front of the toilet. A pinching sensation pierces my head and everything goes black again.

I cough against the smoke, flames licking at my doorway, and there is nowhere to go.

"Amy!

"Mom! I'm in my room!"

"Stay there. We're coming for you."

195

I wait, and the sounds of the fire eating away at wood have my bones rattling. "Mom?"

Nothing.

"Mom?"

She screams and I suck in smoke at the horrific, blood-curdling sound, coughing with the impact and trying to cry her name.

"Mom!" I finally manage. "Mom!"

She's still screaming. And screaming. "Mom!"

"Amy!"

My brother's voice rips through the hallway and the hell I am living, bringing with it hope. "Chad! Get Mom! Help Mom!"

"Listen to me, Amy," he shouts, but all I hear is my mother, still screaming.

"Mom! You have to help her. Chad, help her!"

"Listen the fuck up, Amy. I can't get to you. Go to the window."

"Mom!" I shout.

"Amy, damn it, go to the window or you are going to die."

Die. My mother is dying. I want to go to her but the flames climb closer, inside my room. On wobbling legs, I go to the window.

"Are you at the window?" Chad shouts.

"Yes. Yes."

"Open the window and jump."

I do it. I open the window and look down into the darkness below. "It's too high."

"You were a gymnast for years."

"Who quit because I was afraid of heights!"

"Jump, Amy, and make it count. Do it."

My mother is no longer screaming. My mother is—

"No!" I shout. She can't be dead. "I can't jump. I can't jump."

"Jump, Amy. Jump now or I will come through the flames and die trying to get to you."

I gasp. "I'll jump. I'll jump." I climb out of the window and I look back toward the flames and then forward. I hold my breath and jump.

Chapter Twenty

$$\pi$$

A my. Amy. Wake up. Please, baby. Wake up."
I blink through a sticky sensation on my face. "Liam?"
"Yes. Thank God. You scared the hell out of me." He
grabs a towel and presses it to my head.

I focus on the red stains on his light gray t-shirt. "I'm
bleeding?"

"You hit your head and cut it open. We need to get you to
the ER."

I grab his arm. "You're here. How are you here?"

"Yeah, baby, I'm here and I shouldn't have left you alone."

Any reply I might have had is lost to the roll of my stomach.
"Oh," I gasp. "I'm going to be sick." I grab for the toilet and
Liam holds my hair back and manages to keep the cloth on my
head as I embarrassingly throw up. "I really don't want you to see
me like this."

"Nonsense. Can you hold the towel to your head so I can get
you some clothes?"

"Yes." I take it from him. "I'm good. You're sure I need
stitches?"

"One hundred percent."

I squeeze my eyes shut against the sound of my mother's
screams echoing in my mind. And I hear Chad calling my name.
Amy. Amy. But I wasn't Amy then. I was Lara. Why was he
calling me Amy? Is my mind trying to tell me something, or am I

so removed from my past that there is nothing but Amy left? Jump. Jump now.

"Amy." I jump at Liam's hand stroking down my hair. "Easy. Are you okay?"

"Yes." But I'm not. I want to tell him everything. I want to tell him more than I want my next breath, but that nightmare has reminded me how very real the danger I am in is, and I am not clearheaded enough to decide what that means for him. For us. "I'm dizzy."

"I'm guessing you have a concussion. Can you stand up so we can get you dressed?"

"Yes." He helps me to my feet and I feel pathetic when he has to practically put my shorts on me and then tie his shirt at my waist. He drops sandals at my feet and I slide into them. He puts the toilet seat down. "Sit. Let me call for a car service before we head downstairs."

Ten minutes later we exit the hotel and the doorman pulls open the passenger door of a black sedan for me. My head is spinning and my stomach is queasy and Liam helps me into the car.

"Amy. What the hell?"

Liam and I both turn to find Jared standing there. "Did he touch you?" He glares at Liam. "You son of a bitch, did you hit her?"

"No!" I exclaim. "No. Jared, I fell."

"Back the fuck off," Liam growls. "I would never touch her, but I will you."

"Amy?" Jared asks, and he seems sincerely worried. "Did he touch you?"

"No. I told you no. He wasn't even here when it happened. He just flew into town and found me passed out."

"Let's go," Liam orders me. "Blood is seeping through the towel. You need those stitches."

"I'm fine, Jared, but thank you." I slide into the car and Liam follows, shutting us inside. He taps the seat and gives the driver directions. I have never wanted to block out the rest of the world as I do right now. He turns to me and his eyes are dark shadows and turbulence. I expect him to ask about Jared but he doesn't.

"You aren't going to ask about him?"

"You're hurt. It's not time for fifty questions."

"I thought the game was twenty questions."

"I have fifty but I won't ask tonight."

But he wants to, and now that the miles are no longer between us, I'm not letting Jared get there instead. "I ran into him at the coffee shop today, but other than that this is the first I've seen of him since that night at Earl's."

"I didn't ask."

"You wanted to."

"Yes. I wanted to."

"I'm glad you're here. You didn't tell me you were coming back."

"I didn't want to promise something I couldn't make happen. I wrapped everything up as I'd hoped early today. The woman my father put in the intensive care unit was moved to a regular room and I took care of all of her medical expenses and set up a trust fund for her daughter." He grimaces. "My father also moved, from jail to rehab."

"You're a good man, Liam. I don't know why you doubt that."

He leans in and kisses me, his voice softening, rough like gravel. "I couldn't sleep last night thinking I'd get back here and you'd be gone."

"I promised I'd be here."

"And I promised I'd hurry back." He reaches up and holds the towel for me. "We have a lot to talk about."

"Yes," I agree. "Yes, we do." And not for the first time, I wonder if Liam knows more than I think he does.

"Right now, I just want to get you healthy." He pulls me close and my hand settles on his heart. It thrums beneath my palm, a soothing melody that feels like home. He feels like home. I'm going to tell him everything. I just have to find the right time.

***

I wake on my side, a bright blast of sunlight illuminating the room, and my eyes lock on the sight of Liam standing in the bathroom knotting a red silk tie at his neck. He's been back for two days, one I regretfully slept through, the other we spent in bed together, but today he goes back to war with his "a-hole" investor. We haven't talked. Not really. I was too sick from the concussion and he was too protective to do anything but worry about me. Despite the ER giving me a thumbs-up on a clear CT Scan, Liam is determined to get me to a neurologist, but I know he'll understand why I won't go when I finally tell him about my past. Or what I know of it.

Liam's gaze suddenly lifts and catches on mine in the mirror, and my stomach flutters wildly. He gives me a devastatingly sexy smile, and turns to close the distance between us. And I am like a starving animal soaking in his male grace and the way the gray pinstriped suit accents his long, leanly muscled frame.

"How do you feel?" he asks, sitting on the edge of the bed.

I sit as well and touch the small bandage at my hairline, one that thankfully has been downsized from gigantic the day before. "Ready to be out of bed." I stroke my hand down his arm. "Or to stay in it with you here." I glance at the clock and note the nearly one o'clock hour. "But alas, you must go, and I have the acupuncturist showing up in an hour."

"Call me after the appointment and let me know how it went. I hate leaving you."

"I'm fine and you need to take care of business."

"I'll make it fast, if I can."

A few minutes later he is gone, and I shower and dress before heading to the mini-kitchen off the dining room area to make coffee. The instant I bring the table into view I go still at the sight of my notepad and computer. I didn't expect Liam to be back and I never put my things away.

I walk to the table and sink down into the chair in front of my computer. My screensaver is on and my notepad is closed, but I open it to see what would be the first thing Liam would have seen if he had as well. I've scribbled Why is there no record of the fire? and Who covered it up?, both phrases underlined heavily. There are references to my hometown papers and my father's name is everywhere. I feel sick to my stomach all over again and it has nothing to do with my concussion.

Liam may never have looked at these notes, but if he did, he is too smart not to put two and two together. I have to talk to him now. I have to make sure he doesn't do anything to get the wrong people's attention. I dial his cell. He doesn't answer. I press fingers to my forehead. He never answers his phone.

A text beeps and I quickly glance at it. Just walked into meeting. Are you okay?

I sigh and type. Yes. Yes I'm fine.

Derek wants us to go to dinner with him and Mike.

Mike is the "a-hole". I'm never going to get to talk to Liam at this rate. What time?

Seven. I'll send a car for you.

I'll be ready.

***

At seven sharp I exit the hotel in a white, form-fitting lace dress Liam had picked out during our shopping trip, paired with red high heels and a red purse, both of which I'd chosen. My only other accessory is the white bandage by my hairline that, despite my efforts to sweep my long blonde hair over it and seal it there with hairspray, still shows.

I'm barely in the car when my cell phone rings, and it's Meg. I frown. She's avoided me for almost a week and she chooses now to call? "Hello."

"I just ran into Jared. He told me you had some sort of a head injury? He said he'd stopped by the hotel several times and left you messages you won't reply to."

Jared stopped by the hotel? "I've been in bed. I had a concussion."

"Was it—"

My defenses prickle. "No, it was not Liam. Jared knows that. Is Luke back in town?"

"Oh, yes. I emailed you a new property list. Did you see it?"

"No. No, I didn't."

"Luke inadvertently sent you the wrong one and he apologizes. He let your boss know. I guess you were supposed to do some reports you haven't done. Dermit was asking why, so you better get on it."

I'm confused. Completely confused. Who do I work for? Do I work for anyone? Is Dermit real or not? "Can you please get me a number for my boss?"

"You'll have to talk to Luke about that."

"Can I make an appointment?"

"I'll get with him and call you."

My phone beeps. "I need to take that. I'll check in tomorrow." I click over to Liam.

"Where are you?" he asks.

"I'm almost there, I think. I'm in the car."

"I'll be at the door waiting on you."

"Okay. Yes." We end the call and I immediately pull up my email. The only email is from Meg with the property listing. I really have no idea what is a cover story and what is a problem anymore. The idea of telling Liam everything and no longer being on my own with this sounds better every second.

"Your destination, ma'am," the driver says, and the door opens almost immediately. Liam leans in and tosses a large bill at the driver. "Keep the change."

He offers me his hand and pulls me to my feet, giving me a hot head-to-toe inspection before leaning in near my ear. "You look good enough to eat. I think I will."

"Liam," I gasp softly, instantly warm all over, my nipples tightening. That is how easily this man gets to me.

Deep, sexy laughter rumbles in his chest and he shuts the door behind me. "Come with me." He laces my fingers with his and pulls me toward the building, and the way he has said the words "come with me" has me quaking with the certainty he is up to something naughty.

We enter the high-rise building and my heels click on the fine white ceramic tile that blends with my dress and contrasts with my shoes. I glance upward at spiraling rows of offices that remind me of a corkscrew and seem to climb forever. "Wait," I say, and tug on Liam's hand.

He stops and turns to me, glancing up as I am, and then back down at me. "You like it?"

"This is the building you designed, isn't it?"

"Yes. This is it. You like it?"

"It's…" I struggle for a word that suits it, and settle on, "sexy. Like you."

He pulls me against him. "Sexy, huh?"

"Yes. Very." My fingers curl on his cheek. "And brilliant, also like you."

His eyes darken and heat. "Come with me," he orders again, and sets us in motion.

We step onto the elevator and though I know the building is tall I gape at the panel that reads 107 floors. "107 floors?"

Liam punches in a code and then directs us to the top floor. "Yes, 107."

"That's an intimidating elevator ride."

He molds me close. "I'll protect you," he vows, and I'm not sure he's talking about the elevator ride. I'm not sure anything is what it seems ever in my world.

"Why 107?"

"105 had been done and seven is lucky."

"You believe in luck?"

"You don't?"

"Not really."

"We ended up seated together on a plane. I'd say that's pretty lucky."

I soften inside, and more of that warmth he stirs in me pools low in my belly and slides hotly between my thighs. "I think my luck is changing." The car jumps a little and I jump with it. "Or not. What was that?"

"The car stops at floor one hundred and shifts to the right slightly."

"I don't think I want to know why."

"It's part of the sway built into the top of the tower." The elevator stops. "And just that quick, we're here." The doors slide open and I'm more than a little glad to get the heck off the car after that jump, planned or not.

We exit into a hallway and Liam indicates another elevator. "The last two floors require another ride up, but I want to show you something first."

"Aren't we going to be late to dinner?"

"I told you 7:00 and them 7:30."

We travel a narrow hallway with glass windows from floor to ceiling and I feel a bit dizzy and unsteady. Liam opens a huge wooden door and motions me inside. I step into an oval-shaped room that is nothing but windows and random pairs of leather chairs split by small tables.

Liam takes my hand and I always have this sense he is worried I am about to run away. But I'm not running from him. It's time he knows I'm running to him. He leads me to the far side of the room and it is like I am standing on a cloud staring down at buildings twinkling like stars. "It's beautiful."

"So are you," he murmurs, his body framing mine from behind.

"You know," I say, turning in his arms, "Mike might have some merit with the whole 'tallest building' idea. He knows you won't make it just another tall building."

"He knows he wants the tallest building. Period. The end."

He turns me and sets me down in a chair, going down on a knee in front of me and sliding my skirt up my thighs. I look over my shoulder. "No one is going to catch us," he assures me. "I locked the door."

He cups my sex and suddenly jerks on my panties, ripping them away. I gasp. "Liam!"

He laughs and shoves them in his pant pocket. "Now I have something to think about while ol' Mike runs his mouth." His hands stroke back up my thighs. "It's been too long since I've been inside you."

My cheeks heat at his boldness, but I agree. "Yes."

"Did you take a pregnancy test?"

I'm taken aback by the unexpected question. "I told them I might be at the hospital."

His lips curve. "I did, too."

"You did?"

"Yes. Did they test you?"

"Yes. But they said it was too soon to be accurate."

"When can you tell?"

"I think another week."

"Call the doctor and ask."

I nod. "I will."

"Tomorrow."

"Yes. Tomorrow."

"I'm going to give us both something else to think about over dinner." He slips two fingers into the V of my body.

"Liam," I gasp. "Not here."

"Yes. Here." And before I can object again, his head is between my thighs and his tongue laps at my clit. I mean to object. Really I do, but his fingers slide inside me and he is licking me in that way he does that drives me insane.

I grab the arms of the chair and Liam pushes the skirt of my dress higher, lifting one of my legs to his shoulder. For a moment, I drink in the image of me sitting in the chair with this gorgeous man between my legs and me spread wide for him, and it is erotic and exciting, like everything with Liam. Pleasure spikes, already building in some deep spot in my sex and I swear I just keep on being the easiest orgasms this man has ever given anyone. He touches me and I shudder. He licks and I moan. And that is just what happens. He licks me again, I moan, and then my sex clenches around his fingers. I shatter like glass thrown to the ground, instantly, and in tiny little pieces, pleasure splintering through every nerve ending in my body, until I am limp in the chair.

I blink the image of my leg over his shoulder into view and blush furiously. I try to pull it down and he leans in and licks me one last time. I shudder with the impact and he chuckles, then settles my leg on the ground. I quickly try to shimmy my skirt down my legs, and can't get it.

Liam pushes to his feet and pulls me with him, caressing my dress back into place.

"I can't believe we just did that here."

He leans in and kisses me, pressing his tongue into my mouth, before he whispers, "And now we can both have a taste of what the rest of the night will hold. Mike be damned."

Chapter Twenty-One

$$\pi$$

The restaurant is a circle that rotates and has a bar in the
center with spectacular views of the city. Liam and I join
our group of what will be six, including us, and Mike, Mr.
A-Hole himself, greets me with a handshake. Mike is as Liam has
described: rather short for a man, no taller than my five feet, four
inches, forty-something, and otherwise quite decent looking. I say
a quick hello to the others attending the dinner and we all are
seated. Mike to my left. Liam to my right. Derek on the opposite
side of Mike, and two other investors on the far side of the table.

The first order of business is wine, which I refuse for fear I
might be pregnant. "Diet whatever you have," I say, and Liam
squeezes my leg, pulling my gaze to his, and there is awareness
and approval there. And heat. Lots of heat. I think the idea of me
being pregnant actually turns him on. But I think all men get a
macho rise out of the idea of creating a baby on some level. That
doesn't mean they're happy when the round belly and dirty
diapers come around.

"So tell me about yourself, Amy," Mike encourages.

"I'm a boring secretary," I reply, automatically slipping into
deflection mode. That's who I am, deflection girl, and I am so
ready to change that. "I'd much rather hear about you," I
continue. "Were you an investor in this spectacular building Liam
designed?"

Derek laughs, drawing my gaze. "Glad you're along for
dinner, Amy." He nods to Liam. "Good call."

Liam squeezes my leg. "I couldn't agree more."

"She certainly knows how to start things out with a bang," Mike concedes, "but she makes my point. This building is spectacular. Let's do it again a little bigger."

"But you're creating a place that is more than a workspace this time," I argue. "You're creating a small city, from what I understand."

"This building is more than a workspace."

"A pyramid—"

"Is Las Vegas fodder for tourists," Mike finishes for me.

"Tell that to the Egyptians who spent years creating just one of the structures. Tell that to the many scientists and experts who spend year after year trying to figure out how it was even possible for an ancient society to build the structures. And do you really think Liam would build something that would be Vegas-like unless he was creating it for Vegas?"

Mike gives me a hard look, glances at Liam, and then back at me. "Okay Amy," he conceds with a smile, "you have a point. Considering the masterpiece of a building we are sitting inside at present, I cannot say I think Liam would do anything that wasn't spectacular."

I grin my approval and a waitress appears. Once she takes our orders, the conversation shifts to the stock market for what seems like forever. Even if I understood any of it, Liam's hand stroking my leg isn't allowing my brain to work, and no matter how many times I clamp down on his fingers, he sets them in motion again, each time tugging my dress a little higher up my thigh.

Dessert time finds Derek and Liam in deep conversation with the opposite side of the table, and Mike and I restart our conversation about buildings. Mike points out the many amazing buildings around the world that are record-breaking heights, or were, when first built. I quickly remind him that he is forgetting the many amazing structures that get attention for uniqueness, rather than height.

When Mike is without any true knowledge of the miracle of pyramids, I glance at Liam and Derek, confirming they are still distracted, before I dare to dare to be a tad more liberal about my knowledge of the subject. .

"I wonder," I say, after we've talked a good hour in which Mike appears genuinely enthralled by the mysteries and the creation of the pyramids, "if you could incorporate a museum into the project your building and get non-profit funding to offset the expense."

I lean back in my seat and suddenly realize that Derek and Liam are gone and I didn't even know they left. "If you're just a secretary," Mike announces, "you're a wasted commodity."

"I, ah, thank you." I stare at the empty seats, feeling a frisson of unease. "Excuse me if you will, Mike. I'm going to run to the ladies' room." I push to my feet and waste no time rushing away, scanning for Liam and Derek, and decide I'll take a trip to the bathroom and use the privacy to call Liam.

I'm about to head into the bathroom when I hear Liam's voice coming from a balcony just opposite where I'm standing. I move in that direction and stop dead when I hear, "Did you get the data off her computer?"

"All of it," Derek says. "Including the camera."

"So the camera feed is live?"

"Hot as a day in Texas. Are you sure you have her under control?"

"I can handle Amy. You just get me what I need."

The word "Texas" rolls around in my head several times and hits me like a hard punch in the gut. I bolt, my heart is in my throat, adrenaline surging through me to the point where I'm shaking. I arrive at the elevator and punch the button a good ten times until it opens, and I all but lunge inside the car. I hold my breath, waiting for the doors to close, certain I will be discovered. When finally the car is moving, I inhale deeply, willing my pulse to slow so I can think. This doesn't mean Liam is the bad guy. It doesn't. Maybe he dug into my past. Maybe he's trying to help me. But why would he film me? Why? Why? Why? I was falling in

THE SECRET LIFE OF AMY BENSON

love with him. I am in love with him. The idea that he and I were nothing but a facade cuts me deeply. I want to believe in him and us, but I do not dare risk trusting him. I have to survive first, and I need a plan.

Think, Amy. Think. You have to get out of here. Leave the state. Leave tonight. The elevator opens on the bottom floor and I know there are cameras everywhere, easily tracking my departure. I run through the empty lobby and ignore the security guard behind the desk, exiting the building and immediately cutting to my right. I pause momentarily to remove my shoes before running several blocks until I spot a cab and hail it.

I climb inside. "Where to, lady?"

Where to? Where to? My cell phone rings and I am smart enough to know that not only can the GPS chip be used to follow me, Liam has the money to make it happen. With my heart in my throat, I roll down the window and toss the phone outside, my thoughts bouncing all over the place with my emotions. I need a fake ID I can't get until tomorrow. And I need to be close to Evernight so I can try to reach my handler one last time.

I lean forward to talk to the driver. "There's a hotel called Cherry Creek Inn, in Cherry Creek North. Take me there." I hesitate, then add, "But stop by a twenty-four-hour Walmart first." I need supplies and a cash machine.

Forty-five minutes later, I step into the hotel room I've paid for in cash with Liam's words playing in my head. Run to me, Amy, not from me. Angrily, I swipe at the tears that slip down my cheeks. I'm not going to cry over him. I'm not. I'm not going to cry at all.

I dump the contents of my shopping bag on the bed. A cheap pair of tennis shoes, a couple of tank tops and pairs of shorts, a few toiletries. I remove the wad of cash from my purse that I pulled from Liam's credit card and toss it down as well. Tomorrow I'll clean out my New York accounts, get a fake ID to travel with so that Amy Bensen will never be traceable as leaving town, and then I'm gone.

"I'm not running at all, Liam," I whisper. I'm going back to Texas.

The End....

Look for the exciting conclusion of The Secret Life of Amy Bensen 'INFINITE POSSIBILITIES' very soon.